ELIZABETH SOPHIA TOMLINS,
THE VICTIM OF FANCY (1786)

CHAWTON HOUSE LIBRARY SERIES:
WOMEN'S NOVELS

Series Editors: *Stephen Bending*
                      Stephen Bygrave

TITLES IN THIS SERIES

FORTHCOMING TITLES

Sarah Green, *The Private History of the Court of England*
edited by Fiona Price

Riccoboni and Brooke, Graffigny and Roberts, *Translations and Continuations*
edited by Marjin S. Kaplan

Elizabeth Sophia Tomlins,
The Victim of Fancy (1786)

EDITED BY

Daniel Cook

Routledge
Taylor & Francis Group

LONDON AND NEW YORK

First published 2009 by Pickering & Chatto (Publishers) Limited

Published 2016 by Routledge
2 Park Square, Milton Park, Abingdon, Oxfordshire OX14 4RN
711 Third Avenue, New York, NY 10017, USA

First issued in paperback 2016

Routledge is an imprint of the Taylor & Francis Group, an informa business

BRITISH LIBRARY CATALOGUING IN PUBLICATION DATA

Tomlins, Elizabeth Sophia, 1763–1828.
The victim of fancy. – (Chawton House library series. Women's novels) 1.
Women–Education–Fiction. I. Title II. Series III. Cook, Daniel. 823.6-dc22

ISBN 13: 978-1-138-23558-8 (pbk)
ISBN 13: 978-1-8519-6259-4 (hbk)

Typeset by Pickering & Chatto (Publishers) Limited

CONTENTS

ACKNOWLEDGEMENTS

Many thanks are due to Stephen Bygrave and Stephen Bending for their encouragement of the project. Polly Stevens Fields's work on Elizabeth Tomlins has been especially useful. I am also grateful to Antonia Forster and David A. Brewer for their aid and advice and to Sandy White and the staff of the Chawton House Library for their help with materials. I'd also like to thank Mark Pollard, Eleanor Hooker, and everyone at Pickering & Chatto for their patience and understanding throughout. Finally, I'd like to thank my students at Newnham College, Cambridge for giving me some wonderful insights into their own experiences of reading this novel. Makes a change from Austen, they said.

INTRODUCTION

In 1785 Elizabeth Sophia Tomlins produced her first novel, *The Conquests of the Heart*, anonymously, as the work of 'a young lady'. By the end of 1786, when she completed *The Victim of Fancy*, she graduated to the more grown-up sobriquet of 'a lady'. She was still only twenty-three years old. Nonetheless, many contemporaries shared the endorsement given in the obituary notice of Tomlins in the November issue of the *Gentleman's Magazine* for 1828, in which this youthful work is described as 'the most popular of all [her] performances'.[1] Far from peaking in the 1780s, however, Tomlins went on to produce two other substantial novels: *Memoirs of a Baroness* (1792) and *Rosalind de Tracey* (1798). She also wrote a steady ream of poems in a variety of styles and forms, the quality of which, according to the *Gentleman's Magazine*, fully 'entitles her to notice'.[2] Her early verse, like much of her later work, reverberates with such ennobling themes as equality, personal liberty and virtue. Alongside her best-known poem, 'The Slave', she produced a striking ballad trilogy of love, betrayal and death: 'Connal' (1782), 'Mary' (1783) and 'Athol' (1784). In 1797 she collaborated with her older brother, Thomas Edlyne Tomlins, on *Tributes of Affection*, a collection of verse which critics reviewed somewhat lukewarmly.[3] The collection includes 'E's 'To Eliza; gardening' (1790), a tribute to 'S' written in terms consonant with Tomlins's own preoccupation with the fleeting attractions of maidenhood:

> The Maid unconscious of her pow'r,
> Unconscious of the fleeting hour,
> Still wastes, unkind and heedless Fair,
> '*Her* sweetness on the desert air'.
>
> While lost to joy her Lover sighs,
> And like the drooping flow'ret dies:
> But ne'er must hope like that to prove
> ELIZA's fond regret and love.[4]

Aged twenty-seven at this point, Tomlins had become, by some eighteenth-century standards, an old maid.[5] Yet, not unlike Theresa Morven, the heroine of *The Victim of Fancy*, Tomlins was considered to be both beautiful and talented and not without suitors. And, not unlike her heroine, her intellectual pursuits were affected, for better and worse, by domestic concerns. Her background was relatively well-to-do and financially secure. Her father, Thomas Tomlins, worked 'upwards of fifty years' as a solicitor and clerk to the Company of Painters-Stainers, a position later held by his son and his grandson, Frederick Guest Tomlins, who also worked as a publisher and a playwright.[6] The education and career of Thomas Edlyne Tomlins, the eldest son, is well documented: admitted as a scholar at St Paul's School in 1769, he then entered Queen's College, Oxford in 1778, before he was called to the bar in 1783. He was knighted in 1814.[7] Although nothing is known about Elizabeth Tomlins's education, she is remembered fondly for her 'intellectual superiority', as evidenced by the large number of references to canonical and fashionable literature throughout her works. She also worked on translations, including the 'first History of Napoleon Bonaparte', and contributed regularly to 'nearly every respectable periodical' of the age.[8] For seven years prior to the death of her father in 1815 Tomlins found the time and energy to superintend the family's 'professional concerns' as well as to educate her sisters. Modern scholars have largely overlooked her mother, even though she features prominently in the obituary notice in the *Gentleman's Magazine*: Tomlins's 'vivacity and tenderness of disposition – distinguishing features of her character – were fostered by the correct taste of an excellent mother'. Although evidently she was highly devoted to her family, and to her brother Thomas and three younger sisters in particular, the *Gentleman's Magazine* insinuates that her 'noble spirit of devotion' was borne out of obligation to a patriarch 'whose severe notions of duty led him to receive the sacrifice only as a right'.[9]

These domestic restrictions on her creativity notwithstanding, Tomlins clearly benefited from the political connections made by her father and the literary friendships of her brother. As the obituarist in the *Gentleman's Magazine* observes, Tomlins became 'acquainted with many persons of talent of that period, who, through their intercourse with her father professionally, were introduced to her society'.[10] Her brother Thomas worked as an editor of the *St. James's Chronicle*, a popular daily newspaper printed by the Baldwin family, and the *Whitehall Evening Post*.[11] The connection with the Baldwins is of particular significance. Not only did the *St. James's Chronicle* advertise *The Victim of Fancy* on two occasions, the novel appeared under the imprint of R. Baldwin of Paternoster Row, along with G. and T. Wilkie of St. Paul's Churchyard.[12] These strong literary and political connections aside, *The Victim of Fancy* is in part an elaborate allegory about the difficulties of achieving genuine critical acclaim in the literary marketplace. The heroine of the novel is caught up in and questions various fashionable hero-worships of, most persistently, the pan-European cult of Werther, but also of Sophia Lee, author of *The Recess*, Frances Burney, Ossian, Milton and William Hayley. In the company of Burney, Charlotte Lennox, and other well-known novelists, Tomlins examines the perils as well as the pleasures of modern reading and, indeed, polite society at large.

I.

The Victim of Fancy is dedicated to William Hayley, a poet characterized here as a patron of women artists, the 'female band', as Tomlins puts it (p. 5). Hayley, according to his modern biographer Morchard Bishop, 'at once accepted the dedication'.[13] This seems to have been fairly common practice for Hayley, who famously encouraged Charlotte Smith, an aspiring poet and novelist as well as a mother of a large brood and a wife to a spendthrift in the 1780s. Having left her husband, Smith wrote a number of much admired sonnets, which were initially rejected by James Dodsley, the major publisher of English poetry at the time. In despair she appealed to a neighbour with literary renown, Hayley, who allowed her to dedicate to him a quarto volume of her works, *Elegiac Sonnets, and other Essays*, which did in fact eventually appear under Dodsley's imprint in 1784. The collection was hugely successful and ran to five editions in as many years. In the dedication Smith acknowledges Hayley as 'the greatest modern Master' of essays in verse form.[14] In preparing her own dedication to Hayley, Tomlins perhaps had in mind a small section in the fourth epistle of *An Essay on Epic Poetry* (1782), in which Hayley lauds the merits of Britain's female poets, particularly Anna Seward, the 'leader of the lovely train'. While lamenting that hitherto Prejudice has forbidden 'Female hands to touch the lyre', Hayley praises the 'Fair-ones' who are seeking to 'cancel such absurd decrees'. He entreats them to

> Proceed, ye Sisters of the tuneful Shell,
> Without a scruple, in that Art excel,
> Which reigns, by virtuous Pleasure's soft controul,
> In sweet accordance with the Female soul;
> Pure as yourselves, and like your charms design'd
> To bless the earth, and humanize mankind.[15]

Thankful of such encouragement, Tomlins responds in kind:

> She from the raptures of a youthful heart,
> Tho' "not an artist, yet a friend to art,"
> Would mark how woman venerates thy lays,
> And trembling add, ennobled by thy praise,
> A leaf of myrtle to thy wreath of bays! (p. 5)

True to her expressed desire to celebrate the master, Tomlins's novel is replete with allusions to Hayley's works, principally his recent *Essay on Epic Poetry*, a work much admired by Smith, Seward, Helen Maria Williams and other prominent women of letters.

The form in which Hayley's works appear in *The Victim of Fancy* ranges from the odd colourful if inconspicuous phrasing to a group of lines that seem to articulate the heroine's mood. In either case the presence of Hayley's writings marks out Theresa's seemingly unreflective endorsement of a patriarchal literary heritage, albeit one palliated by the sweet virtues of the female band. As per convention this heritage includes Shakespeare, Homer – though Theresa weeps over her inability to read his works in Greek – and the 'divine' Milton, who, somewhat oddly, is singled out as a neglected literary genius: 'I have kissed the neglected receptacle of the bones of Milton; I have wetted his grave with the enthusiastic tears of admiration' (p. 12).[16] As Jacqueline Pearson has observed, Milton's *Paradise Lost* was widely treated as a touchstone for 'female taste and virtue' in the eighteenth century, as with More's Lucilla Stanley, Kett's Emily, Clementina in *Sir Charles Grandison* and Adeline in Radcliffe's *The Romance of the Forest*.[17] By 1787 Mary Wollstonecraft was 'sick of hearing' derivative praise for Milton, Pope and Shakespeare from those female readers 'anxious to have the reputation of taste'.[18] Not unlike the eponymous heroine of one of the most influential epistolary novels of the period, Samuel Richardson's *Clarissa* (1748), Theresa peppers her letters with quotations from Milton's works, principally *Paradise Lost* and *Comus*. In spite of her insatiable (and almost debilitating) appetite for knowledge beyond her scope, such as Greek-language literature, Theresa conforms to a number of well-established educational guidebooks aimed at young women. For instance, in *Letters on the Improvement of the Mind* (1773), Hester Chapone recommends the reading of history, poetry (especially Shakespeare, Milton, Homer and Virgil) and moral philosophy. Crucially, however, she advises that 'the greatest care should be taken in the choice of those *fictitious stories*, that so enchant the mind – most of which tend to inflame the passions of youth, whilst the chief purpose of education should be to moderate and restrain them'.[19]

In contrast to her veneration of a patriarchal literary heritage Theresa routinely questions the value of modern novels by women – Chapone's 'fictitious stories' – or, more accurately, she is anxious that they measure up to the standards of established authors. In a key scene in the Pump Room at Bath the heroine (almost) finds herself in the company of Sophia Lee, recent author of *The Recess* (1783–5), a popular historical and Gothic novel.

> We were scarce entered before I perceived the universal attention which was attracted, and in a moment the name of *Lee* circulated in a whisper [...] And this then, thought I, is the *Temeraire*, whose name has been publicly joined with that of one of the first female writers of our age! My prepossession for her vanished; since who, my dear brother, is there that should be ranked with the writer of Cecilia? There is a strength of mind and nobleness of sentiment pervading that whole work, which has often forced tears from my eyes, and has warmed and enraptured my heart. I wished,

however, to address this celebrated author; but Mr. S—— joined us, and, before my attention was again disengaged, she was so much surrounded, I could not think of breaking through the circle she had attracted, and Burell, too anxious for my health, staid not till it was dispersed. (p. 36)

In this hurly-burly scene Theresa barely catches a glimpse of Lee, whom she describes as the *Temeraire* – the audacious one – as her recent success had marked her out as a much sought-after literary celebrity. In particular Theresa questions whether Lee deserves to be ranked alongside Frances Burney, the author of *Evelina* (1778) and *Cecilia* (1782). As Tomlins would have been aware, Burney had become by the late 1780s 'a standard against whom new women novelists were measured', in the words of Jane Spencer.[20] Such was the case with Charlotte Smith's first novel, which showed 'little inferiority' to Burney's work, according to the *Critical Review*.[21] Theresa here assumes that Lee fails to reach the same standards.

Eventually she does indeed get to read *The Recess* during a three-day convalescence, and she is astounded by 'that elegant work, in which is united all that is most charming to the heart and the imagination!' 'Its language', she continues, 'conveys images the most enchanting to the fancy, and scenes the most interesting to the heart' (p. 56). Duly captivated, Theresa finds that she cannot put the book down:

I was frequently affected even beyond the power of weeping, and scarcely could prevail on my aunt, with all my entreaties, to let me read the last volume: but persuading her that I should, perhaps, be less affected when alone, I had all the luxury of weeping over it by myself. I concluded it some hours before I attempted to rest, and then I started from my dreams, impressed with all the sensations I had felt so strongly in perusing it. (Ibid.)

Towards the end of the first volume of *The Victim of Fancy*, referring back to the Pump Room episode, Theresa concedes that she had responded with 'prejudice and injustice' before reading the book (p. 57). This is offset against the reading habits of an avid if unreflective devourer of 'pretty' literature, Miss C——, who serves as a contrastive foil to Theresa, a delicate and passionate reader struggling to adhere to the reading habits expected of a young girl. In a letter given a few pages after this enthusiastic description of her experience of Lee's novel, Theresa recounts an evening spent playing whist at the house of her aunt's schoolfriend. During the course of the evening 'Miss C—— asked me if I did not think the Recess a pretty thing enough. I was at some loss for an answer; but I conquered myself, however; and said only, 'Yes—" (ibid.). This glib response contradicts Theresa's spirited description in the letter to her brother. Is she shy or inarticulate, or perhaps feeling ashamed? Reading novels, she has been conditioned to believe, is a guilty pleasure.

II.

More naively, Theresa champions what she perceives to be the unappreciated ethical values of the highly controversial novella *The Sorrows of Werter* (1779), the English translation of Johann Wolfgang von Goethe's *Die Freuden des Jungen Werthers* (1774). While other characters discourage her, on the assumption that the book is morally corrupting, she insists on travelling to Bath in order to meet the author, a plot that illustrates both her wide-eyed innocence and her single-mindedness. More broadly Tomlins's novel participates at once in a contemporary craze for 'Werteromania', as the heroine dubs it, and in attempts to palliate the perceived emotional excesses of the novella. A number of British novels and plays in the 1780s exploited the widespread anxiety about the threat of *The Sorrows of Werter*, focusing particularly on the anti-hero's disordered feelings for Charlotte and his resulting suicide. Works such as Edward Taylor's *Werter to Charlotte, a Poem* (1784) and the anonymous *Eleanora: from the Sorrows of Werter* (1785) wore their connections with Goethe's work on their book sleeves. Others, such as *Distressed Virtue* (1781), *Elfrida; or, Paternal Ambition* (1786) and *Sorrows of the Heart* (1787), exploited readers' knowledge of and engagement with the fad. In other novels, such as Herbert Croft's *Love and Madness* (1780), the suicide proved to be a strong point of debate among the characters. The eponymous heroine in Helen Maria Williams's *Julia* (1790), as a final and notable example, comments that Goethe's novella 'is well written, but few will justify its principles'.[22] For a time Werteromania served as a totem for the worst kind of leisured-class excess: luxuriating in literature that was not only unedifying but morally and physically debilitating.

The Sorrows of Werter featured prominently in philosophical debates about the physical and emotional effects of literature on the imagination or, indeed, on the fancy of impressionable youths. In one of her longer juvenile pieces, *Love and Freindship* [sic] (1790), Jane Austen is able to poke fun at the impressionable young girls who used *Sorrows* as a 'handbook for the sensitive heart', in the words of Syndy McMillen Conger, but many prominent literary women, such as Burney and Hannah More, studiously refused to even read it.[23] More in particular savaged the emotionalism of novels like *Sorrow* insofar as such works could be seen as insincere and indulgent. In a later, much revised version of her 1782 poem 'Sensibility' she pointedly attacks the hypothetical woman who 'weeps o'er Werter, while her children starve'.[24] Whereas moralists had taught that 'sensibility could guide people towards greater wisdom, virtue, and happiness', as Conger puts it, *Sorrows* represented a 'counter-demonstration, a nightmare inversion, of the rewards they assumed would fall to those who cultivated happiness'.[25] The moralists were joined by a band of novelists who, as Frank Gees Black demonstrates in his bibliographical study of epistolary fiction in the period, pro-

duced works 'ostensibly to counteract the evils of Wertherism'.[26] In the preface to
The Letters of Charlotte (1786), for example, William James states:

> I am happy that in presenting the following letters to the public, I am not exhibiting
> scenes, or communicating opinions, that can wound delicacy, or pervert sentiment ...
> I am still more sorry that a book so universally read as the *Sorrows of Werter*, should
> fall under this predicament; a book which is not simply an apology for the horrible
> crime of Suicide, but in which, as far as the author's abilities would go, it is justified
> and recommended![27]

This English adaptation parallels the original but, crucially, the point of view
migrates from the 'unbalanced sentimentalist', as Black puts it, to that of the
'healthy-minded Charlotte'.[28] In the Advertisement to *The Victim of Fancy*, Tomlins discusses the public treatment of *Sorrows* in more sympathetic terms:

> whilst the dubiousness of its moral has given rise to the severest censure; the writer
> of the following letters hopes to be excused for endeavouring to bring forward that
> moral in a more favourable, and, she trusts, a more just light, than it has hitherto
> appeared. (p. 6)

In her first letter to her brother, the heroine of *The Victim of Fancy* outlines an
important distinction between Goethe's original text and the supposedly more
moralistic English translation: 'my heart answers not to the name of this Dr.
Goethé; no, it eagerly looks to some child of liberty, to some son of Britain ...
and whoever this author is, he has been misunderstood and abused; he has held
out a moral to mankind' (p. 10). Theresa's suitor Burell is among those who 'misunderstood' the tale and in turn 'strengthened my aunt's unfavourable opinion
of it' (ibid.). The story of Werter, then, frames the ethical grounds upon which
the action of Tomlins's novel revolves. It allows Theresa's guardians to articulate their wish to control her reading and thereby control her intellectual and
moral development. Yet, at the same time, the novella serves as an opportunity
for Theresa to demonstrate her capacity for reasoned argument. In one episode
she enters into a debate with Dr C—— about the usefulness of *Sorrows* as a
cautionary tale for those prone to irrational feeling. In discussing the value of
instructive literature the physician savages those writers who 'subvert every principle which can support society' (p. 43). Holding a copy of *Sorrows* in his hand
he is specifically making an example of the so-called apologist for suicide and
adultery. Amidst much blushing and social embarrassment – as her aunt and
her friends play whist in modest silence – Theresa is compelled to express her
sympathy for Werter:

> Do we not behold in him all that nature and genius can render deserving, wretched,
> forlorn, and ruined by one error, by one passion unconquered, by one wish impru-
> dent only at first unsubdued? There may we not trace every step of the path which

leads to guilt, to misery, to despair, and death? ... We see him, my dear sir, all the powers of his imagination wasted – all the ties of religion subdued in his heart. Alone he stands in the world. (p. 44)

In their obituary notice for Tomlins in 1828 the *Gentleman's Magazine* compares *The Victim of Fancy* favourably with Goethe's novella as the former 'evinced much of the pathos of [*Sorrows*], without the objectionable tendency of its moral'.[29] Likewise, in 1787, the *Critical Review* treats the novel as a mouthpiece for the author's private views: 'A warm admirer of that specious but delusive work, she engages in defence of its moral; and in this respect we find the author, though we hope no child of Fancy, speaks her own sentiments'.[30] In 1787, during a period in which many had fallen under the spell of Werter, the *Gentleman's Magazine* credits Tomlins with a degree of critical perspicacity:

> a very interesting female character is introduced, whose sympathetic feeling with that author seems to have enlightened her to understand what the generality of readers have not discovered, that Werter was insane at the moment of committing the rash action which has justly brought universal censure on that work.[31]

The reviewer delineates more fully the real moral lesson of Tomlins's story:

> It is supposed the moral here intended is, to shew the danger of encouraging that keen sensibility which insinuates into the best minds, and, when encountering a tincture of romance, if not opposed by fortitude, and regulated by a solid understanding, will undermine the constitution, overset the intellects, and, in this example, become *the Victim of Fancy*.

In sum, these reviews rely on two assumptions. The first assumption is that the book is a novelized polemic with which the author seeks to participate in a cultural cleansing of Werteromania. The second relies on the belief that Tomlins treats this mission with the utmost earnestness. The indulgent and somewhat bombastic Advertisement notwithstanding, it is also possible that Tomlins felt, as some of her contemporary novelists felt, that the usefulness of Goethe's youthful work was waning by the end of the 1780s, barely a decade after the work first appeared in English. As an analogous case, in one scene in the second of the four volumes of Charlotte Smith's *Emmeline, the Orphan of the Castle* (1788), the heroine takes up a book 'she had not before opened': *The Sorrows of Werter*. 'She laid it down again with a smile, saying – "That will not do for me tonight".'[32] The heroine in *The Victim of Fancy*, too, seems to lose interest in the novella largely because she is traumatised by Mr S——'s sullen response to her polite rejection of him. Distressed at being the cause of the man's evident anguish, Theresa finds herself 'inclined to think of that Werter, [whom] I have before so warmly admired' (p. 71). Fictitious writing does indeed affect the conduct of impressionable readers, but, as we might infer from this novel, it is young *men* who ought to be sheltered from its powerful effects. In her final letter to her brother, Theresa casually asserts that this 'Werteromania is cured' and embraces instead 'that elegant and durable felicity which is the offspring only of true sensibility of soul, of delicacy and refinement' (pp. 97–8).

Throughout *The Victim of Fancy* Tomlins presents *Sorrows* less as a viable blue-print for a sentimental life than as an outmoded paradigm of a corrupted male emotionalism. This reflected a prominent aspect of the mainstream treatment of Goethe's Werther in England. In focusing largely on the protagonist's fatal passion for Charlotte, the story became a narrowed exposé of the violent excesses of which the 'man of feeling' was capable. This is consistent with Tomlins's use of the Wertherian *topos* in her later work, specifically a verse piece penned jointly with her brother, 'Werter to Charlotte (*Written just before his death*)'.[33] The speaker is keen to exonerate Charlotte, 'Thou guiltless cause of wretched WERTER's end' and insist that it is rather the hero's inability to control his Reason that causes his downfall. The threat of the man of feeling to polite society is also addressed in *The Victim of Fancy* in two substantial ways. Frederick Burell faces the same predicament as Werter: the woman he loves does not reciprocate his feelings and instead loves his close friend (in this case his brother Vincent). But Burell remains a gracious supporter of Theresa and her aunt and, although he speaks about his feelings in highly charged terms, never suicidal. Frank Hyde, Theresa's overzealous admirer, is yet another Wertherian figure. Nonetheless, like Burell, Frank fails to emulate Werter as Theresa bravely thwarts his attempted suicide: 'Swift as thought I darted across the room, and happily secured the pistol, and summoning all my resolution, with one hand, as he wildly seized the other, discharged it' (p. 79). This resembles the heroics of Burney's Evelina, who, observing Macartney's pistols, assumes he is intent on suicide. 'Wild with fright, and scarce knowing what I did, I caught, almost involuntarily, hold of both his arms', she writes, and the 'guilty pistols fell from his hands'.[34] The scene revolves around misapprehension – the pistols are for armed robbery rather than suicide – but nonetheless it is an important moment of self-actualisation for Burney's heroine. Both Evelina and Theresa have to grapple with the weaknesses of masculine sentimentalism in order to validate their own strength.

There are a number of obvious similarities between *Evelina* and *The Victim of Fancy*, no less the epistolary form and the heroines' impressionability, love of reading and fear of sexual advances. Indeed, reviewers of Tomlins's first novel, *The Conquests of the Heart*, had already made connections between the work of Burney and Tomlins, even if disparagingly. *The Conquests of the Heart*, the *Monthly Review* asserted, has 'few claims' to originality because the 'ground work and colouring are evidently borrowed from Evelina and Cecilia'.[35] Nonetheless reviewers of *The Victim of Fancy* instead made comparisons with a novel that remained relatively popular in spite of its age, namely Charlotte Lennox's

The Female Quixote, or, The Adventures of Arabella (1752). A 1787 review of *The Victim of Fancy* in the *Gentleman's Magazine*, for instance, identifies the heroine as 'another female Quixote, animated with equal enthusiasm, differently directed, adorned with every grace, captivating irresistibly every heart, glowing with all the ardour of youthful fancy, in a just cause, endued with sensibility too powerful for her delicate frame'.[36] *The Monthly Review*, similarly, dubs this book a 'new kind of *Female Quixote*', despite conceding that it bears 'no resemblance to any former work of the sort'.[37] The reviewer goes on to discuss the merits of the work: 'We imagine it to be the production of a young Authoress, whose head and heart abound, or rather overflow with sentiment, fancy, feeling, and delicacy, – but all tinctured too strongly with the *extravagant*, and the *romantic*.' *The Town and Country Magazine* concurs with the view that in Tomlins's novel 'sentiment too often usurps the seat of reason'.[38] Conflating the author and her heroine, both reviewers agree that the novel is too extravagant, too bombastic, too sentimental, an interpretation that persisted well into the twentieth century. Theresa's 'excesses blend the noble and the ridiculous', writes J. M. S. Tompkins, 'and she perishes under the wear and tear of her feelings'.[39]

To my mind such readings have long obfuscated Tomlins's subtle examination of divisive social concerns such as the supposedly destructive effect of fictional writing on women of delicate constitutions. By situating Tomlins's work amongst a number of competing literary modes, most notably the British Wertherian novel, the novel of manners, the epistolary form, and the female *bildungsroman*, we can appreciate its value more fully: *The Victim of Fancy* adumbrates the tone and tenor of a number of well-known and largely neglected fictional works and thereby creates a site in which to glimpse the mainstream literary marketplace as it actually existed in the second half of the eighteenth century. Far from saturated with weak-willed romances, it was a thought-provoking if at times overly fussy forum of moral debate.

III.

When the fantasist Arabella, heroine of *The Female Quixote*, finally yields to the authority of public reason in the shape of a clergyman she is readied for the unromantic but proper life of a good wife. After a series of comic mishaps and misrecognitions, Burney's Evelina, not unlike Fielding's Tom Jones, finally marries, too. This resolution, however, has polarised modern critics. In John Richetti's reading *Evelina* is 'an eighteenth-century fairy tale with a Cinderella and a Prince Charming', whereas Kristina Straub argues that marriage is figured here 'as both the means of escape from female maturity's hardships and an institution that formalizes and justifies those hardships'.[40] Despite their opposing conclusions, both critics identify a tension within Burney's treatment of the patriarchal society that characterized the period. Similarly, the heroine's entrance into polite society in *The Victim of Fancy* is unsettled by the author's ideological uncertainty. While Tomlins is careful to draw a distinction between 'uncontaminated religion' and the hypocrisy of individual churchmen, the institution of religion is associated with confinement (p. 92). Theresa finds herself 'totally confounded' by the two-facedness of the curate Mr Manville as he 'expressed a regard for the young man, whom a minute before he had represented as despicable and profligate, pressed him to stay with all the apparent earnestness of friendship' (p. 24). And, perhaps with a small nod to the oppressiveness of religion in the Gothic tradition, we are reminded on a handful of occasions that the heroine had been incarcerated in a nunnery by a wicked stepmother.

Theresa learns to distinguish true from false religion and yet cannot comprehend that she is the victim of another invasive institution: the family. Even though it was her aunt, Deborah Carlton, who liberated Theresa from the nunnery at the insistence of her brother, Colonel Morven, they also control her. As Ruth Perry has pointed out, brothers featured prominently in a number of mid-century novels as moral compasses and, in the absence of fathers, 'were expected to protect their sisters' chastity'.[41] Stationed in Gibraltar during the American revolutionary wars, Morven is largely absent during the action of the novel. And, although Theresa addresses her letters to him, none of his replies are given directly. In his place Theresa's aunt fills the parental role under Morven's strictures, assisted by the ever present Burell. Aunts, as Perry has it, are often figured as a 'bracing tonic' in eighteenth-century fiction.[42] Learned, wise and mature, they serve as handmaids to the young heroine's integration with polite society. Intent on marrying her off, Theresa's aunt frequently counsels the heroine on how to act, especially around men: 'Theresa, says my aunt, when women talk of their love of learning, half of the men charge it to affectation only; and, what is worse, when they believe it real ... they at once envy and despise us for it' (p. 12). This conforms to the matter-of-factness of Dr Gregory's advice in his *Legacy to his Daughters* (1774): 'If you happen to have any learning, keep it a profound secret, especially from the men, who generally look with a jealous and malignant eye on a woman of great parts and cultivated understanding'. In 1792, largely in response to Gregory among others, Mary Wollstonecraft savaged the 'herd of novelists' who glorified the 'romantic unnatural delicacy of feeling' and thereby wasted 'their lives in *imagining* how happy they should have been with a husband who could love them with a fervid increasing affection every day, and all day'.[43]

Tomlins seemed rather to be among a band of women novelists who had grown weary of the long-established archetype of the fictional heroine promoted by Samuel Richardson and his followers from the 1740s onwards. Richardson's Pamela, in the words of the author, is 'an affectionate *Wife*, a faithful *Friend*, a polite and kind *Neighbour*, and indulgent *Mother*, and a beneficent *Mistress*'.[44]

In the decades after *Pamela* women authors wrote with increasing scepticism of the interdependence of these roles. Two prominent novelists, Mary Hays and Helen Maria Williams, suffered ridicule for associating with men who were not their husbands, while Charlotte Smith and others had failed marriages. As Janet Todd has argued, this coincided with a migration away from 'eulogies of wifeliness towards the glorification of the mother'.[45] While she does not entertain the possibility of marriage in her letters, Theresa's hopes of marrying a man whom she has come to love dearly and sincerely, Vincent, the younger brother of Burell, are dashed. Soon inseparable from Vincent, she stops writing to her brother because 'I shall have no time to spare to my pen' (p. 97). (It is noted in passing that her compliant and unreflective counterpart, Miss C——, has recently married.) However, in the ensuing narrative – a collocation of Ruth's story and some remaining letters from Theresa and others – we learn of the deaths of her brother (from war wounds) and her aunt (from grief). And, with her societal pillars removed, she follows them to the grave. Even though the heroine insists that 'we are formed for each other', the love of Vincent is not enough to secure her a so-called fairytale wedding, it seems (p. 95). We might take this as the tragedy of the story: just at the point at which Theresa can accept that she must turn from selfish pursuits to marriage, she dies. Or alternatively we might argue that 'this too attractive young man' is too much of a literary cliché to work, an interpretation reinforced by his numerous and often misguided attempts at chivalry, one of which almost results in his death (p. 81). In this reading the tragedy is that life and the ghastliness of war fails to measure up to the fantasy of books.

On her deathbed towards the end of *The Victim of Fancy* Theresa concedes that the 'impetuosity' of her passions 'has done much in destroying me' (p. 107). Wishing to impart the wisdom learned in her short life she advises her close friend Ruth how best to raise her young daughter Sophy: 'let her learn to regulate the passions, even the most innocent of her heart' (ibid.). In many ways Sophy is a younger version of Theresa. Both are instinctively compassionate: Sophy for her fellow May Day revellers, Theresa for Joannah and her wounded bother, the young ensign Villers. While other narratives have petered out, specifically the protagonist's impassioned search for the author of *The Sorrows of Werter* and her aunt's obligatory attempts to marry her off, this heartfelt and pragmatic speech gives resolution to a plot that had been stifled throughout the novel. On a number of occasions Theresa laments that her correspondence with Ruth, a young mother whom she greatly admires, has not been reciprocated. This runs counter to 'a large number of epistolary novels in which', as April Alliston points out, 'the primary fictional correspondences are exchanged between female characters'.[46] We eventually learn that sexual jealousy has been the cause of their ruptured exchange. Frank, the would-be suicide, has left Ruth in frenzied pursuit of Theresa and thereby the Wertherian plot tramples over Tomlins's attempts at a conventional epistolary exchange between women. Instead Ruth completes the novel by providing her own narrative at the cessation of There-sa's letters, along with some stoical correspondence between the Burell brothers. The fairytale ending expected by avid readers of sentimental fiction is thereby unravelled.

By redacting the novel's happy ending – be it a wedding or the safe return of the heroine's beloved brother – Tomlins engaged with an increasing trend among novelists towards questioning the multiform role of women in society. Theresa Morven is not a wife, daughter, or mother. Nor is she the reader she wishes to be. Barely glimpsing Sophia Lee and soon weary of Werteromania, she is caught between a literary life she cannot join and a social world unwilling to accommodate her intellectual and moral development. *The Victim of Fancy* is, then, an elaborate exploration of individual and familial responsibilities and, as such, it is deservedly ranked as Tomlins's greatest work.

Notes

1. *Gentleman's Magazine*, 98 (1828), p. 471. This obituary had already appeared with some variations in the *Monthly Magazine, or, British Register*, 6:33 (1828), p. 322.
2. Ibid.
3. See *Analytical Review*, 26:2 (1797), pp. 166–7 and *The Critical Review*, 26 (1799), p. 109.
4. *Tributes of Affection: with The Slave; and other poems. By a lady; and her brother* (London: printed by H. and C. Baldwin for T. N. Longman and C. Dilly, 1797), p. 69. The advertisement announces that the works attributed to 'S' are by Elizabeth (Sophia) and the works under 'E' by Thomas (Edlyne).
5. See J. B. Kern, 'The Old Maid, or "to Grow Old, and be Poor, and Laughed at"', *Fetter'd or Free? British Women Novelists, 1670–1815*, ed. M. A. Schofield and Cecilia Macheski (Ohio: Ohio State University Press, 1987), pp. 201–14 (p. 202).
6. *Gentleman's Magazine*, 98 (1828), p. 471. See P. Stevens Fields, 'Tomlins, Elizabeth Sophia (1763–1828)', *Oxford Dictionary of National Biography* (Oxford, 2004). Here-after cited as *ODNB*.
7. E. I. Carlyle, 'Tomlins, Sir Thomas Edlyne (1762–1841)', rev. Jonathan Harris, *ODNB*.
8. *Gentleman's Magazine*, 98 (1828), p. 471.
9. Ibid.
10. Ibid.
11. *Gentleman's Magazine*, 16 (1841), pp. 321–2.
12. See J. Raven and A. Forster, with the assistance of S. Bending, *The English Novel 1770–1829: A Bibliographical Survey of Prose Fiction Published in the British Isles; Volume 1: 1770–1799* (Oxford: Oxford University Press, 2000), 1787:51.
13. M. Bishop, *Blake's Hayley: The Life, Works, and Friendships of William Hayley* (London: Victor Gollancz, 1951), p. 319.
14. C. Smith, *Elegiac Sonnets, and other Essays* (Chichester: printed by Dennett Jaques; sold by Dodsley, Gardner, Baldwin, and Bew, 1784), p. vi.

15. *An Essay on Epic Poetry; in five epistles to the Revd. Mr. Mason. With notes* (London: J. Dodsley, 1782), pp. 75–6.

16. In a poem written in 1795, Tomlins praises Milton, the 'matchless Bard! whose ever-during name / Thy Britain's pride, her wonder, and her joy', *Tributes of Affection*, p. 67.

17. J. Pearson, *Women's Reading in Britain, 1750–1835: A Dangerous Recreation* (Cambridge: Cambridge University Press, 1999), p. 58-9. For an account of a counter-tradition see Sandra M. Gilbert, 'Patriarchal Poetry and Women Readers: Reflections on Milton's Bogey', *PMLA*, 93:3 (1978), pp. 368–82.

18. *Thoughts on the Education of Daughters: with Reflections on Female Conduct, in the more Important Duties of Life* (London: J. Johnson, 1787), p. 52.

19. *Letters on the Improvement of the Mind, Addressed to a Young Lady* (London: printed by H. Hughs for J. Walter, 1773), vol. 2, p. 144. Emphasis in original.

20. *The Rise of the Woman Novelist: From Aphra Behn to Jane Austen* (Oxford: Basil Blackwell, 1986), p. 98.

21. *The Critical Review*, 65 (1788), p. 530.

22. *Julia, a novel* (London: T. Cadell, 1790), vol. 2, p. 202.

23. 'The Sorrows of Young Charlotte: Werther's English Sisters 1785–1805', *Goethe Yearbook*, 3 (1986), pp. 21–65.

24. This version of the text is taken from *The Works of Hannah More, in Four Volumes: including several pieces never before published* (Dublin: D. Graisberry, 1803), vol. 1, p. 92.

25. Conger 'The Sorrows of Young Charlotte: Werther's English Sisters 1785–1805', *Goethe Yearbook*, 3 (1986), pp. 21–65.

26. F. G. Black, *The Epistolary Novel in the Late Eighteenth Century: A Descriptive and Bibliographical Study* (Eugene, OR: University of Oregon, 1940), p. 24.

27. *The Letters of Charlotte, during her Connexion with Werter* (London: T. Cadell, 1786), vol. 1, pp. i–iii.

28. Black, *The Epistolatory Novel*, p. 25.

29. *Gentleman's Magazine*, 98 (1828), p. 471.

30. *Critical Review*, 63 (1787), p. 107.

31. *Gentleman's Magazine*, 57 (1787), p. 519.

32. *Emmeline, the Orphan of the Castle* (London: T. Cadell, 1788), vol. 2, p. 129.

33. The piece is unsigned. A footnote reads: 'This and the following piece were written by S. and E. as a sort of trial of skill; in which it is not difficult to imagine who was vanquished: but they are left unsigned to exercise the sagacity of the Reader', *Tributes of Affection*, p. 125n.

34. *Evelina, or, a Young Lady's Entrance into the World. In a Series of Letters* (London: T. Lowndes, 1779), vol. 2, p. 96.

35. *The Monthly Review*, 74 (1786), pp. 472–3.

36. *Gentleman's Magazine*, 57 (1787), p. 159.

37. *The Monthly Review*, 76 (1787), pp. 446–7.

38. *Town and Country Magazine*, 19 (1787), p. 123.

39. *The Popular Novel in England, 1770–1800* (London: Methuen & Co Ltd, 1932), p. 100.

40. *The English Novel in History 1700–1780* (London and New York: Routledge, 1999), p. 229; *Divided Fictions: Fanny Burney and Female Strategy* (Lexington, KY: University Press of Kentucky, 1987), pp. 53–77.

41. R. Perry, *Novel Relations: The Transformation of Kinship in English Literature and Culture, 1748-1818* (Cambridge: Cambridge University Press, 2004), p. 153.
42. Perry, *Novel Relations*, p. 348.
43. M. Wollstonecraft, *A Vindication of the Rights of Woman: with strictures on political and moral subjects* (London: J. Johnson, 1792), p. 63. Emphasis in original.
44. S. Richardson, *Pamela; or, Virtue Rewarded* (London: S. Richardson, 1741 [1742]), vol. 3, p. ii.
45. J. Todd, *Sensibility: An Introduction* (London and New York: Methuen, 1986), p. 112.
46. A. Alliston, 'The Value of a Literary Legacy: Retracing the Transmission of Value through Female Lines', *The Yale Journal of Criticism*, 4:1 (1990), pp. 109–27 (p. 109).

SELECTED BIBLIOGRAPHY

Biography

Anon., 'Miss Tomlins', *The Gentleman's Magazine*, 98 (1828), p. 471.

Anon., 'Miss Tomlins', *The Monthly Magazine, or, British Register*, 6:33 (1828), p. 322.

Carlyle, E. I., 'Tomlins, Sir Thomas Edlyne (1762–1841)', revised by Jonathan Harris, *Oxford Dictionary of National Biography* <accessed May 2009>.

Fields, P. S., 'Tomlins, Elizabeth Sophia (1763–1828)', *Oxford Dictionary of National Biography* <accessed May 2009>.

Povey, K., 'Elizabeth Sophia Tomlins', *Notes & Queries*, 154 (18 February 1928), pp. 115–16.

Reviews of *The Victim of Fancy*

Critical Review, 63 (1787), pp. 107–9.

English Review, 14 (1789), p. 469.

Gentleman's Magazine, 57 (1787), p. 159.

Monthly Review, 76 (1787), pp. 446–7.

New Lady's Magazine, 2 (1787), p. 151.

Town & Country Magazine, 19 (1787), p. 123.

Secondary Material

Alliston, A., 'The Value of a Literary Legacy: Retracing the Transmission of Value through Female Lines', *The Yale Journal of Criticism*, 4:1 (1990), pp. 109–27.

Anon., *Biographium Fæmineum. The female worthies: or, memoirs of the most illustrious ladies, of all ages and nations* (London: printed for S. Crowder, J. Payne, et al., 1766).

Anon., *The Progress of Fashion: exhibiting a view of its influence in all the departments of life* (London: J. Sewell, 1786).

Anon., *The Sorrows of Werter: a German Story* (London: J. Dodsley, 1779).

Balderston, K. C. (ed.), *Thraliana: The Diary of Mrs. Hester Lynch Thrale* (Oxford: Clarendon Press, 1942).

Beattie, J., *Poems on Several Occasions* (Edinburgh: W. Creech, 1776).

Bishop, M., *Blake's Hayley: The Life, Works, and Friendships of William Hayley* (London: Victor Gollancz, 1951).

Black, F. G., *The Epistolary Novel in the Late Eighteenth Century: A Descriptive and Bibliographical Study* (Eugene, OR: University of Oregon, 1940).

Bray, J., *The Female Reader in the English Novel: From Burney to Austen* (New York: Routledge, 2009).

Bruce, M., *Poems on Several Occasions* (Edinburgh: J. Robertson, 1770).

Burney, Frances, *Cecilia; or Memoirs of an Heiress* (London: T. Payne and Son, and T. Cadell, 1782).

—, *Evelina, or, a Young Lady's Entrance into the World. In a Series of Letters* (London: T. Lowndes, 1779).

Chapone, H., *Letters on the Improvement of the Mind, Addressed to a Young Lady* (London: printed by H. Hughs for J. Walter, 1773).

Conger, S. M., 'The Sorrows of Young Charlotte: Werther's English Sisters 1785–1805', *Goethe Yearbook*, 3 (1986), pp. 21–65.

Cunnington, C. W. and P. Cunnington, *Handbook of English Costume in the Eighteenth Century* (London: Faber and Faber, 1957).

Dryden, J., *The Indian Queen: a tragedy. Written by the Honorable Sir Robert Howard, and Mr. Dryden* (London: J. Tonson, 1735).

'E. S. J.', *The Scientific Magazine, and Freemasons' Repository* (London: George Cawthorn, 1797).

Falconer, W., *The Shipwreck. A Poem. In Three Cantos. By a Sailor* (London: A. Millar, 1762).

Forster, A., *Index to Book Reviews in England 1775–1800* (London: The British Library, 1997).

Genlis, S.-F. Ducrest de, *Adelaide and Theodore, or Letters on Education*, ed. G. Dow, Chawton House Library Series (London: Pickering & Chatto, 2007).

—, *Tales of the Castle*, trans. Thomas Holcroft (London: G. Robinson, 1785).

Gilbert, S. M., 'Patriarchal Poetry and Women Readers: Reflections on Milton's Bogey', *PMLA*, 93:3 (1978), pp. 368–82.

Gracián, B., *The Hero*, trans. 'a Gentleman of Oxford' (London: T. Cox, 1726).

Hayley, W., *An Essay on Epic Poetry; in five epistles to the Revd. Mr. Mason. With notes* (London: J. Dodsley, 1782).

—, *An Essay on History; in three epistles to Edward Gibbon, Esq.* (London: J. Dodsley, 1780).

—, *Triumphs of Temper* (London: J. Dodsley, 1781).

Hoy, J., *Poems on Various Subjects* (Edinburgh: Macfarquhar and Elliot, 1781).

Hoyle, E., *A Short Treatise on the Game of Whist* (London: John Watts, 1742).

James, W., *The Letters of Charlotte, during her connexion with Werter* (London: T. Cadell, 1786).

Johnson, S., *The Poetical Works of Samuel Johnson* (London: G. Kearsley, 1785).

Kern, J. B., 'The Old Maid, or "to grow old, and be poor, and laughed at"', *Fetter'd or Free? British Women Novelists, 1670–1815*, ed. Mary Anne Schofield and Cecilia Macheski (Ohio and London: Ohio State University Press, 1987), pp. 201–14.

Lee, S., *The Recess, or, A Tale of Other Times* (London: T. Cadell, 1783–5).

Mason, W., *Elfrida, a dramatic poem* (London: J. and P. Knapton, 1752).

Milton, J., *Comus, a Mask: (now adapted to the stage) as Alter'd from Milton's Mask at Ludlow-Castle, which was Never Represented but on Michaelmas-Day, 1634; before the Right Honble. the Earl of Bridgewater, Lord President of Wales* (London: printed by J. Hughs, for R. Dodsley, 1738).

—, *Paradise Lost: A Poem, in Twelve Books… A New Edition, with Notes of Various Authors, by Thomas Newton* (London: J. and R. Tonson and S. Draper, 1749).

More, H., *The Works of Hannah More, in Four Volumes: including several pieces never before published* (Dublin: D. Graisberry, 1803).

Pearson, J., *Women's Reading in Britain, 1750–1835: A Dangerous Recreation* (Cambridge: Cambridge University Press, 1999).

Percy, T., *The Hermit of Warkworth; a Northumberland Ballad. In Three fits of Cantos* (London: T. Davies, and S. Leacroft, 1771).

Perry, R., *Novel Relations: The Transformation of Kinship in English Literature and Culture, 1748–1818* (Cambridge: Cambridge University Press, 2004).

—, *Women, Letters, and the Novel* (New York: AMS Press, 1980).

Raven, J., and A. Forster, with the assistance of S. Bending, *The English Novel 1770–1829: A Bibliographical Survey of Prose Fiction Published in the British Isles; Volume 1: 1770–1799* (Oxford: Oxford University Press, 2000).

Richardson, S., *Pamela; or, Virtue Rewarded* (London: S. Richardson, 1741 [1742]).

Richetti, J., *The English Novel in History 1700–1780* (London and New York: Routledge, 1999).

Schofield, M. A., and C. Macheski (eds) *Fetter'd or Free? British Women Novelists, 1670–1815* (Ohio and London: Ohio State University Press, 1987).

Smith, C., *Elegiac Sonnets, and other Essays* (Chichester: printed by Dennett Jaques; sold by Dodsley, Gardner, Baldwin, and Bew, 1784).

—, *Emmeline, the Orphan of the Castle* (London: T. Cadell, 1788).

Spencer, J., *The Rise of the Woman Novelist: From Aphra Behn to Jane Austen* (Oxford: Basil Blackwell, 1986).

St Clair, W., *The Godwins and The Shelleys: A Biography of a Family* (Baltimore, MD: The Johns Hopkins University Press, 1989).

Straub, K., *Divided Fictions: Fanny Burney and Female Strategy* (Lexington, KY: University Press of Kentucky, 1987).

Todd, J., *Sensibility: An Introduction* (London and New York: Methuen, 1986).

Tompkins, J. M. S., *The Popular Novel in England, 1770–1800* (London: Methuen & Co Ltd, 1932).

Turner, C., *Living by the Pen: Women Writers in the Eighteenth Century* (London and New York: Routledge, 1992).

Williams, H. M., *Julia, a novel* (London: T. Cadell, 1790).

Wollstonecraft, M., *Thoughts on the Education of Daughters: with Reflections on Female Conduct, in the More Important Duties of Life* (London: J. Johnson, 1787).

—, *A Vindication of the Rights of Woman: with Strictures on Political and Moral Subjects* (London: J. Johnson, 1792).

NOTE ON THE TEXT

For this volume I have used the Chawton House Library copy of the first and only edition of *The Victim of Fancy*. Another copy is housed in the Ohio State University Library. The date of the text is given as 1787 on the title page, but it was advertised as for sale in the 19-21 December 1786 issue of the *St. James's Chronicle*. This periodical was in the hands of the Baldwin family, a well-known clan of prolific booksellers. *The Victim of Fancy* appeared under the imprint of R. Baldwin of Paternoster Row, in conjunction with G. and T. Wilkie of St. Paul's Churchyard. It was priced 5 shillings, sewed, according to *The Monthly Review* and the *St. James's Chronicle*; 6 shillings according to *The Critical Review*. The novel is a small octavo book in two volumes bound in one (Vol. 1, [iv], 186pp, Vol. 2, 152pp). The Chawton House Library copy is taken from the John Charles Hardy collection and bears his bookplate as well as a contemporary armorial bookplate in the name of William Smallbone.

In preparing the text of this edition I have intervened as little as possible. Discrepancies in the spelling of proper nouns, such as Mr. Manville and Joannah have been corrected. Unusual spellings and grammatical forms (especially past tenses), including solecisms ('you was'), have been retained on the whole. I have retained 'shewn', 'ideot', 'compleatly', 'encreased' and other such spellings as they can be found in a significant range of contemporary writings or in the Oxford English Dictionary. Although I have sought to render the text consistent, I have allowed variations of the same word, such as honoured/honored and increase/encrease, even when they appear in close proximity. This is in keeping with common eighteenth-century printing practices. Obvious misspellings or very unusual usages, such as 'Embarassed' and 'forbode' respectively, have been silently corrected. Some words have been silently corrected to avoid unnecessary confusion. I have followed the punctuation of the original edition, but in order to aid the reader I have inserted inverted commas to indicate direct speech (rather than paraphrased or indirect speech) and quotation marks around all lines of quoted text. (This might seem a little odd in the case of an epistolary novel but I hope it is more useful than not). In the few instances in which quotation marks are used for direct speech in the original text these have been changed to inverted commas here. I have regularised the otherwise distracting em dashes and hyphens.

THE
VICTIM OF FANCY.

VOL. I.

THE

VICTIM OF FANCY,

A NOVEL.

IN TWO VOLUMES.

BY A LADY,

Author of the CONQUESTS of the HEART.

VOL. I.

With frames and constitutions weaker than Men have, the passions of
Women are warmer; and the rays of their genius concentrate to the
object on which they engage themselves more strongly – it absorbs all
other considerations.

PROGRESS OF FASHION.[2]

LONDON:

Sold by R. BALDWIN, Pater-noster row; and
G. and T. WILKIE, St. Paul's Church-yard.
MDCCLXXXVII.

DEDICATION.

To WILLIAM HAYLEY, Esq.[3]

HARMONIOUS bard of "Britain's living choir,"[4]
Whose skilful fingers touch the potent lyre;
Whose precepts, whilst they charm the soul, improve,
And point each footstep to the goal you love;
Say, shall the candour of thy noble line,
Which says to Woman, "Poesy is thine,"
And bids, with dauntless aim, the female band[5]
Pluck the green laurel from the Muses hand –
Rest all unnotic'd by one grateful lay,
Unsung by those to whom you point the way?
And shalt thou, Hayley, whose melodious strain
Darts emulation thro' each glowing vein,
And fondly pays to fame and genius true,
The fair Comnena's shade[6], the tribute due,
Whilst thy fair pages female worth retrieve,
Shalt thou no tribute from the sex receive?
Yes – whilst with homage throb a thousand hearts,
Lo! from the throng the bold adventurer starts;
Her cheek yet wet with admiration's tears,
And awed by genius which her soul reveres,
From motives, sacred as thy breast might own,
Her flowers she brings to thy poetic throne:
Simple and few, whilst at thy feet she strews
The warm effusions of a female muse,
She from the raptures of a youthful heart,
Tho' "not an artist, yet a friend to art,"[7]
Would mark how woman venerates thy lays,
And trembling add, ennobled by thy praise,
A leaf of myrtle to thy wreath of bays!

ADVERTISEMENT.

AS those striking traits of originality and spirit, which mark the work called THE SORROWS OF WERTER, have excited attention and admiration almost universal, whilst the dubiousness of its moral has given rise to the severest censure[8]; the writer of the following letters hopes to be excused for endeavouring to bring forward that moral in a more favourable, and, she trusts, a more just light, than it has hitherto appeared. She should esteem herself amply rewarded, might she hope to succeed in her attempt to wipe off the blot which tinges those beautiful pages; and she has only to wish, that, whilst endeavouring to render justice to acknowledged genius, and to regulate the principles of the heart, she may have been able to engage its affections, and to point out to it, as the most desirable of all blessings, Religion and Virtue.

She is not without some fears that the dedicating this trifle to such a name may be considered as a presumption; but she begs leave to remark, that the ancients, when they brought their offerings to the altar of Apollo, did not believe their presents in themselves worthy the acceptance of the "master of the lyre,"[9] but each, according to his capacity, laid them at his feet as a token of homage due to their inspirer, and of the consciousness they felt of his superiority.

THE
VICTIM OF FANCY.

FREDERICK BURELL, *Esq. to Major* MORVEN, *at* Gibraltar.[10]

My dear Friend,

WHEN I quitted you and embarked for France, you may remember I had no intention of making any stay in that kingdom; but my unexpected meeting with my brother, who was lately arrived there in his return from Italy, detained me longer than I had intended: you cannot, I imagine, have forgotten Vincent[11]; and he bade me assure you that he remembers and respects you as a friend; and congratulates you on the particular, as well as general glory which you have acquired in the service you so gallantly engaged in. It was in tenderness to his mother only, that he relinquished his own predominant desire of being a soldier; and since her decease, warm as I know him to be with loyalty and valour, the peace which prevails in Europe has happily taken from him the possibility of indulging or signalizing the noble fire of his disposition; for the meanest soldier you have commanded there is to him an object of envy. He now intends passing some time at the French Court, where he is respected in a manner peculiarly flattering: but as many affairs called me to England, I quitted him after passing three weeks at Paris, leaving behind me a few grave cautions befitting an elder brother. My first care on my arrival in London was to fulfil the commission with which you had entrusted me; my credentials soon introduced me to your sister, and I have the satisfaction to find from her conversation, that what you so much wish to keep secret, has not yet transpired. You desired, at parting, my opinion of her, supposing she must be much altered in your three years absence, which have been almost wholly devoted by her to improvement. What she was when you left her, just released from a nunnery, where an interested step-mother would have buried her, it is impossible for me to tell – beautiful she must ever have been, and as soon as I saw her my heart pronounced her the most charming woman I had ever beheld. Can I say more, than, that joined to the most captivating figure, she possesses all the elegant accomplishments in a superior degree, in an age and country where they are almost universal? I shall ever think myself indebted to you for having announced me to her in the favourable light of your friend, since in ten minutes conversation, I found there could be no other half so pleasing to her. To that favour also I owe your aunt's admitting my visits with peculiar complacency, which, since the first, have been pretty frequent. When I told your sister the dangers with which you have been surrounded, the tears which stole through her long and dark eye-lashes, shewed the tender interest which she takes in her brother; and she thanked Heaven for your escape, with an earnestness which moved me so much, that I was scarce able to proceed. I soon found that she acknowledges her obligations to you, with the same nobleness of generosity with which you attempt to conceal them. Tremble for me, Morven, since to the softest appearance of feminine delicacy, she joins an animation and energy, believe me, superior to every thing I have before seen, and I caught myself at first sitting in silent surprise, contemplating the unusual and enchanting combination.

Your aunt doats on her; I find I have recommended myself to the good lady, by the sentiments which have sometimes escaped me in your sister's absence. She has rendered herself mistress of the Italian, and in the learned languages has made a considerable progress, by an assiduity which has distinguished her in all her pursuits. The desire of knowledge in her, your aunt remarks, almost becomes a passion; but a man who loved her, would know there is another much stronger than that in the world, and would hope too, that such a mind as hers was destined some day or other to experience it. Perhaps this letter may make you suspect that there is at least one such man, and that there should be thousands would be no more than justice. I have the happiness of seeing her very often; but, alas! if she should hereafter be as deaf, as she is at present blind to my affection, I shall find no security but in flight. I think you will at least not be my enemy in this affair, and I don't desire any thing further: I know what she thinks of her obligations to her brother, and with all my friendship I would not be indebted even to you, for her acceptance of me as a lover. At present I am received both by her and your aunt with friendship, and admitted into their parties without reserve. I so much dread to forfeit these privileges, that, however painful the effort, I shall impose a long silence on myself, at least to your lovely sister. – I see too plainly an application to study in her which your aunt complains of, and shall make it my endeavour to dissipate her attention a little, if possible. Would to heaven I dare flatter myself, that, in endeavouring to be of service to her, I might advance by imperceptible steps toward my own happiness! – As you desired me to express freely my sentiments of your sister, and her situation, I will mention to you what strikes me as an error in your aunt's kindness, and which has given me some uneasiness. Your aunt reads but little herself – but she leaves the world of books open to your sister. Her taste and native delicacy, it is true, will prevent her from perusing any work which strikes her as inconsistent with pure morality and virtue; yet I cannot but fear lest her lively imagination should mislead her; since whatever she peruses, she enters into with a warmth of disposition, which from the first I have observed in her. I am strengthened in this opinion by her being charmed with a production which has lately fallen into her hands, concerning the author of which there has been some uncertainty. He has been censured with severity by some, and your sister, who thinks this censure unjust, stands forth as a champion in his cause[12]; entering with such earnestness into the idea of his being injured, that, within these few days, she has expressed a desire of discovering and conversing with him, so earnestly indeed, that I feared lest it should amount to a resolution, and almost offended her by treating the execution of it as a jest. If she should persist, permit me, dear Morven, to supply your presence to her; suffer me to attend and protect this intelligent pupil of fancy, in whose conduct I find myself interested more than equally with yourself. I know your friendship for me will make you excuse the freedom of this confession, and I only offer mine for you, as an apology for it. I intreat you to believe that I remain, more firmly than ever,

Yours sincerely,
FREDERICK BURELL.

LETTER II.

Miss MORVEN *to Colonel* MORVEN.

YOU accuse me of enthusiasm! – you my brother who yet wander with the ardor of a soldier on the rock of Gibraltar, and have dedicated your life to the hero who defended it – you, in short, who have delivered from the devouring gulph of superstition a sister, whom the voice of interest would have sacrificed! – Be the period of that enthusiasm and of my existence but one, and I will never complain. – For twenty years immured from all that the heart pants after, from knowledge and even from nature; like a bird from its prison my soul bursts from confinement: awakened from the darkness of ignorance, I behold the face of creation: I hear the voice of genius, my heart vibrates to its sound: I now first feel that I exist; in the rapture, yet new to my heart, I spring forward; I rejoice in this my happier birth-day, I look on the first moment of being as infinitely less dear:

my mind is no longer benighted; all the rays of intelligence pour in at once upon my soul, and I am happy.

My dear brother, independent of the world as you have made me, why should I blush to avow to that world my passionate admiration of the sublime effusions of science or sensibility? – From that admiration it arises that I have formed a wish which my aunt and your friend Burell combat in vain – I have read and admired Werter, and I would be ascertained of its author and his principles. I don't know how it is, but my heart answers not to the name of this Dr. Goethé; no, it eagerly looks to some child of liberty, to some son of Britain, for the author of that animated expression, that overwhelming tenderness, that frenzy of sensibility which those interesting pages display: and whoever this author is, he has been misunderstood and abused[13]; he has held out a moral to mankind, and they turn their eyes away, and behold it not. – What would I give to remove the veil that obscures it, to stop the malignancy of that blast which may tarnish even the laurels of the writer of Werter! – The fire of genius, the charms of nature, painted as they are by his hand, even they, had he forgotten the ties of religion and the duties of society, would merit nothing but oblivion. My aunt blames this work which has enchanted me, she blames me also for defending it, and I have, for once, the happiness of being named with its author. Burell has just now left me; we talked of Werter; unfortunately he has strengthened my aunt's unfavourable opinion of it. Should the day ever come when I can confute them from the mouth of its author, I will not promise to use my triumph with moderation.

LETTER III.

FOR fifteen days have I watched incessantly over my dear aunt, she was suddenly seized with a fever, and her recovery was doubted. In the moments when reason ceased to enlighten her mind, in the wildness of that affection, which still throbbed at her heart, the name of your sister hung on her lips: what did I not before owe to her tenderness? Through her means was it known that I was not the ideot I had been represented. Through her was I brought to the arms of that brother to whom I owe more than existence. Our hearts warm'd with similar affections, our minds glowing with all the ardor of youth, to know and to love each other was the same. Perhaps I ought not to say there is no love which can equal, but can I allow that any can surpass that of a sister? – I knelt by her on the couch of sickness, I poured forth my soul to the Author of Mercies; in him have I trusted, and she is restored to me.

Her fever was contagious; but be not alarmed; I am recovered. The bloom which you flattered is faded, but my heart is unalterable; it still beats for you; it is still open to the impressions of genius and sensibility.

LETTER IV.

MY aunt's recovery, thank heaven, is almost perfected: my own is less rapid in its progress, and I am yet debarred that application which has enabled me, in a time comparatively short to the period of education, to store my mind with the seeds of science, and ennoble my heart by the study of virtue. I feel myself much obliged by the interest which Burell has taken in my aunt's indisposition, and my own. His solicitude for those allied to you, has convinced me of that friendship which he has ever professed to bear you, and which he undoubtedly merits should be returned, in the manner of which you are so capable. He has been here, or rather he is never away. I repeated to him the wish that, before this illness attacked me, had arisen in my mind, and which has not yet subsided there; he again rallied me on it. I believe he pities, he talks of admiring me, but there is something about this fantastical brain of mine, which was never dreamt of in his philosophy. He found me alone, and I could not conceal from him the cause of those tears which then wetted my cheek. You will forgive me when I own they fell with impatience. Alas! it will yet be long, my dear brother, before I can read Homer in the original.[14] 'And is the warmth of that heart', said Burell, 'to be wholly expended on works, though noble, inanimate? And those eyes, expressive of tenderness, shall their rays be directed in search of a being veiled in doubt and obscurity – a being who is perhaps at this minute insensible, while I' – he looked in my face.

I knew that he alluded to my wish of discovering the author of a work which has enchanted me, and I interrupted him with that warmth of disposition which I have not yet learnt to subdue. 'I understand you', said I, 'whilst you can see the passion which hurries me away, and see it in that ridiculous light, which so many will be happy to place it in.' 'It is possible then', exclaimed he, with a sur- prize which I can only account for from the difference of our sensations – 'it is then possible that this one idea so wholly possesses that intelligent mind, that no other can find entrance in it.' I again broke in upon him. 'You mistake me, Burell,' said I; 'one idea does not yet possess me wholly, to the exclusion of all others. You mistake me, I am not yet absolutely mad.' He would have denied the inference, and seemed at a loss for words; but some of those visitors coming in whom nature seems to have thrown into the world just to fill up its vacuum, the conversation ended. I fell in, however, with them upon the reigning fashions – I admired their crapes and their blonds[15], and before they quitted us, they were all of opinion my judgment in those important affairs, might in time be expected to equal their own.

My aunt, who has just left me, came in while I was writing, and glancing her eye over this letter, 'Alas! my dear child,' said she, 'keep secret this ardent desire of knowledge which possesses you so much, or perhaps even this brother will not love you the more for it.' 'And would you infer, Madam,' said I with emotion, 'that he could love me the less?'

With what a sentence did she interrupt me! Were I capable of believing it, I would not transmit it to you: but the heart formed by nature not ungenerous, remains long shut to those severe dictates which age so often dignifies with the name of prudence.

'Theresa,' says my aunt, 'when women talk of their love of learning, half of the men charge it to affectation only; and, what is worse, when they believe it real, by a paradox I cannot solve, they at once envy and despise us for it. To own the truth, learning is a qualification seldom necessary in our sex; and, without extraordinary humility in its possessor, only disgusting – besides that there are a thousand others more conducive to happiness.' – This turn of reasoning is not very consonant with my ideas; but it hurts me the less, as my aunt's frequent complaints of the diligence I am as incapable of abating as she perhaps of approving, points out to me a motive to which to attribute the severity of her reflections.

LETTER V.

I HAVE mentioned to you how much we were indebted to the attention of Burell. Mad as he thinks me, he seems desirous of obliging me, and has shewn it in an instance of which a common mind had been incapable – he has led me to the small grey stone which really covers the ashes of the divine *Milton*[16], and I have wept over it.

How many are there, my brother, who complain that they are confined to one spot of this earth, and that to few it is given to wander over the surface even of this atom, and to pay their devotions at the tombs of those whose names at the distance of ages are repeated with ardor, and whose works are preserved as immortal! yet how many are there who sigh to visit the grottos of Tivoli[17], who have yet forgotten to pay that tribute to the more noble manes of our sublime bard! I have kissed the neglected receptacle of the bones of Milton; I have wetted his grave with the enthusiastic tears of admiration. I have before beheld his bust with pleasure, even where so many imaginary heroes and poets have found place; but the spot which really conceals his last venerable remains, seemed for a moment to infuse his spirit into my breast: I felt superior to the beings which surrounded me, and could almost have fancied that I heard those harps for ever strung, with which he has represented the angels of heaven. I looked on the stone, and my heart felt emotions which I am not able to describe. How often have I lamented, how often hereafter shall I lament, the impossibility of adequately explaining the sensations which arise in my soul! I take the pen in hand; I put my thoughts on paper, and they are nothing. That one idea in Werter, has won me over to admire him, and never may I be an apostate! – So much fire and ease as there is in every line of that work! – Surely we peruse it in its original language, or, like the songs of Ossian[18], the genius of its first author has inspired the nameless translator.[19] How is it that real merit thus shuns the praise which it excites, and, sublimely conscious of its own superiority, hides from the world those brows for which fame prepares a wreath equally honourable and unfading? I yet flatter myself I shall persuade my aunt to suffer me to seek out this doubtful author. If ever, like the generous painter, I shall be so happy as to exclaim, 'I have found him!' how dear will be the spot to my eyes – how sacred the remembrance to my heart!

LETTER VI.

BURELL knows my admiration of painting, that more than speaking sister of poetry[20]; and has promised to introduce me to the galleries of those masters whose names are the glory of our kingdom, of Europe, of the world I will say. – Burell, who I believe loves the arts, knows many of the professors; I shall therefore see their private collections. I have said that I think he pities me – it is a pity, believe me, without contempt – a pity worthy of a good heart, which is only mistaken in its object. I told my aunt so this morning; she answered me only by asking why then I had no pity for him? – 'I!' said I; 'I pity no one for a difference of sentiments; for I am well convinced, that the disposer of hearts has so ordered it, that each rests satisfied with his own, and beholds those of another as a delusion: but it is a pleasing one; and the man who plods over his grounds without one idea but of their fertility, is as jealous of his opinions, and perhaps better contented with them, than the first genius of the universe.' 'Why, my dear girl,' said my aunt, 'you would not have it supposed you neither understand me nor Burell. I am not so easily deceived; I know how penetrating are the eyes of a young woman in such cases.' I did not understand her meaning; but she only laughed at my saying so. We were interrupted, and what she then said, remains as much a riddle to me as ever.

I have been with her to see some of those relations who so obligingly wished to immure me for life.[21] As I quitted them, I pointed them out to my aunt, as a testimony of what I had before advanced. I regard them as objects of pity, while they look on me as no less so. Whispered sentences, tokens of wonder, the epithet fantastical, and others as harsh, frequently escaped them. My aunt would not allow the cases to be similar, and I gained no argument from her but a smile of good-humour, and a half-pronounced something of blindness.

LETTER VII.

WHEN I take up my pen to pour out to you the effusions of my heart, I am most happy; for you, my dear brother, can answer my feelings with that warmth which first enchanted me, and allow for the raptures of a mind new to the pleasures it was formed to taste. The tears, which in these moments wet my paper, will not render me less dear to you: our errors, if they are such, are similar; and those virtues, for which I love you, are reflected, if it be but faintly, in the bosom of your sister.

I have been with Burell, and seen that noble freedom of pencil which marks the works of the British Raphael[22] – the robe flowing to the wind, the animated countenance, the ease, the elegance, the fire, which from the master's hand pervade the warrior panting for battle, or the soft charms of feminine beauty. You, who have delighted to contemplate those enchanting works, and have studied them with an enthusiasm perhaps almost equal to that with which they were at first conceived, will know how to apply my descriptions.

I have seen also, from another pencil – a pencil which speaks to every feeling of the heart – the pale face of the warrior who dies in the arms of his brother heroes. It is imprinted on my memory with a force which no years can efface, and I yet seem to behold the faithful attendant who revenged him. An hour did I contemplate that interesting picture. A lady, who stood near me, kindly directed my attention to the frame, which she assured me cost 150 guineas – the frame, my dear brother, of a picture, and such a picture! – For my part, I had not even seen that it had one.

Do you remember, but I am convinced you do, the works of another son of science sacred to religion and truth. Those faces which ought to be, which, from the hands of the master who undertakes them, are represented as divine. The heart which conceived them, surely, must be filled with ideas of benevolence, of piety, of dignity, and, may I say, of divinity? With what pleasure did my eyes dwell on them! But there is one picture I found in my way which moved and transported me: as I beheld it, my heart melted within me; it addressed itself, it fell prostate before the Eternal; and my spirit, like that of the smiling infant represented there, seemed transporting to the kingdom of God.

Within a few days I have wept on the tomb of Milton; I have since pressed his faithful resemblance to my heart – What would I give, might I but wear it there for ever! "Severe in youthful beauty,"[23] I have seen him, and a century has rolled in vain to prevent me from contemplating his countenance. How frequently do I bow down in thankfulness for my destiny! Had I been used from my infancy to all the treasures of knowledge and all the charms of poetry, I had not known the satisfaction which I now feel. The man who uninterruptedly enjoys the blessings of liberty and peace, feels not that conscious satisfaction which inspires the breast of him who escapes from a dungeon after years of confinement and despair; and what dungeon is there so dark as that of ignorance? – what confinement so drear as that of the mind!

LETTER VIII.

AFTER much entreaty, I have at length prevailed with my aunt, and to-morrow we have resolved to begin a journey which may never have a period; to-morrow I may, perhaps, be some steps nearer to the author of *Werter.* At length this research, which I have so earnestly desired to make, will begin. My aunt will not wholly explain herself, but talks of some hints which she has received, and our first search after him is to be at Bath. With what ardor does my mind spring forward to that invisible goal towards which it so impetuously tends! My heart beats high with a thousand inexplicable expectations, and I vainly endeavour to restrain their impetuosity, by reflecting that they may never be fulfilled.

LETTER IX.

WE have set out and performed our first stage. My aunt is not yet able to travel far at a time, and would persuade me that I am not.

Ought I to inform you that your friend Burell is not well? He has an air of dejection, a look of wearing sorrow that affects me. Ah! my brother, he is your correspondent – How my heart beat, how was every nerve agitated, when I first observed this alteration in his countenance! I looked at him, I would have enquired after you, but the sound died on my lips. He at length understood me; you are well, and I am happy.

Burell has just quitted us, having thought fit to ask my leave to accompany us thus far, and our chaise is now getting ready to proceed. I will own this slow progress agrees not at all with the ardor of my spirit. I feel myself as a painter, who still burns with impatience for the last stroke which shall finish some favourite picture – he sees it grow under his eye, but he fears lest, in the course of the work, some idea should be forgotten. It is with equal warmth that I wish for the moment when my plan shall be compleated, and I shall be satisfied. We have some books with us, but even they will not shorten the way to me. My aunt recommends history to me.[24] I have read history, and what, my dear brother, is it? A picture of the crimes of mankind from generation to generation – too often a false mirror of persons, such as they never existed; while those characters alone worthy of imitation, are frequently lost in the multitude, without even a memorial of their virtues remaining.

LETTER X.

OUR progress is again stopped; yet, would you believe it? I am willing it should be so, and am happy to give up a few days to the knowing of those hearts I have fallen in with.

At this minute we are sheltered in a neat house, where nothing is wanting to convenience, though not much is given to elegance. At the side of my bed, (for I am confined to it,) a little cherub, the picture of health, mirth, and innocence, stands at the knees of her mother, a lovely woman of five-and-twenty, who looks like the mild picture of love and contemplation. I have the happiness to be obliged to this charming woman – But I forget you are ignorant whom I am talking of, and how I became acquainted with them. It was thus:

A few days since, when our chaise was ready, we set out and travelled ten delightful miles. My heart joined in the orisons of the feathered millions that surrounded us; the mild serenity of the morning, the delightful sensation I felt in following the most enthusiastic of my wishes, every thing conspired to render our journey enchanting. For my own part, I could have travelled thus for ever, but my aunt complained of being weary. We stopped at the little village I am yet so near; and whilst she lay down to repose herself, I straggled round it to look for an acquaintance among its inhabitants. At a small distance from the village, and opposite to the low wooden paling of the very house I now write from, I stopped to converse with an old man, who, after spending eighty years of life in labour and penury, is now tottering on its verge. The feebleness of his walk, the few grey locks that covered his sun-burnt temples, attracted my attention and my reverence. Poverty and grief are seldom hard of access. Before he moved his hat I had resolved to speak to him. He has spent his life, as I said, in penury and labour; he complains of injustice and misfortune; he lamented he was no longer able to pursue the track of his youth, and yet he has still hopes of getting better, and is still desirous of living: at eighty years of age he flatters himself with future health, and hopes for that happiness and prosperity which the days of his youth never afforded him. I have observed this, but never before did it strike me so strongly.

I stood contemplating this strange desire of present existence in silence. I had gathered as I stood, without thinking, a wild rose, which hung near me – its leaves fell – the wind carried them away, and not a trace of it remained. I continued to contemplate it as the emblem no less of life than of beauty. The old man seemed to think I was unwilling to listen to him, and had walked away; but I slipped a trifle into his hand, and quitted him, buried in thought. I crossed over and rested on the paling I before mentioned; but on casting up my eyes to the window of the house whose little garden it enclosed, my whole attention was engaged – I beheld a handsome young man, resting his arms on a table which stood near it – I could perceive the animation and tenderness of his countenance earnestly stretched forward – his eyes directed mine to the object on which his attention was fixed. Though half shaded from observation by the window curtain, I saw that lovely woman, whom I have mentioned to you already, the fair mother of the infant now near me: she stood timid, blushing, as if attempting to retire. In the window sat her little girl, busied, with the earnestness of her age, in forming a nosegay of some flowers which lay scattered in her lap. You will think how my attention was engaged. I looked on all three – I wished to be acquainted with them, and in that wish forgot the impropriety I was guilty of in thus stopping to observe them. I do not know when I should have recollected myself, if the little creature, having finished her bouquet, had not hastily risen, and, scattering the remaining flowers on the floor, presented it with the winning grace of innocence to the young gentleman. He took her in his arms, and, what I myself longed to do, almost smothered her with kisses. But her mother approached to take her from him, and then first lifted up her eyes, and beheld me. The blushes on her countenance soon covered me with equal confusion, and I hurried away from the interesting scene. I cast my eyes back a thousand times, in hopes she might have the curiosity to look after me; but I was disappointed, and returned again to the inn at which we had put up, where I found my aunt and dinner waiting for me. I longed, and yet dared not explain myself to her: she would have supposed the whole scene the effects of my wild imagination, as she delights to call it.

How is it, my brother, that there are people, and worthy people too, to whom the book of nature seems opened in vain – that book, every page of which is so sacred to me?

In my last I lamented the slowness of our progress, yet I now myself wished to delay it: but I saw no method of accomplishing it; my aunt for once seemed in haste, and I had no resource left. I found a moment, however, to describe the house to the postillion[25], and desired him to drive near it. My aunt will attempt no more than twenty miles a day; I knew therefore he would move slowly.

We set off, and as we passed the little habitation, I saw the child running on the grass-plat at the door, and strained my eyes, but in vain, in search of some other of the inhabitants. I had even lost sight of her, when I found the chaise overturning. I stretched out my arm over the window, to protect my aunt, and in a minute we were laid in the dust. My injunctions had, I imagine, awakened the postillion's curiosity, and, whilst looking behind him, he drove the chaise wheel on the stump of a tree which stood near the road side, and was not sensible of the mischief time enough to recover himself. The accident was soon perceived: every one near ran to our assistance, and among the rest I beheld the young man who had first attracted my attention. My aunt was unhurt; I had not thought myself much frightened, yet a sickness, unaccountable to me, came over me. With some difficulty I was lifted out of the carriage, and brought into this house; the mistress of which flew to my assistance, but, instead of reviving, I grew yet fainter, and in short, my dear brother, soon discovered my left arm had been broken. A surgeon was sent for, and all is now well: he insists on confining me some days longer; but writing I will not be denied. I have a thousand things more to add; but my aunt, dear woman! too watchful over me, insists on my deferring them for the present. I want to give you a description of my companion, of her little prattler, and of her Frank – I have already learnt his name. My heart labours with a thousand emotions, and I am forbidden to express them.

LETTER XI.

I REPEAT, with pleasure, that I have the happiness to be indebted to the attention of this charming woman. – Peace to those narrow souls who wish never to be obliged! – For my own part, it is my boast that I receive a favour from a noble mind, with a satisfaction even greater than that which I know in conferring one; yet I have felt my heart glow when I have bestowed – it has swelled with sensations on that account which the world should not bribe me to relinquish.

How often do I thank heaven for the exquisite happiness I find myself possessed of, in opening myself to a heart, every pulse of which vibrates to the feelings of my own! That first, that dearest treasure of my life, shall I ever be required to relinquish it? No, my dear brother; the web of my being is more feeble in its texture than yours, and I exist but in the hope of its shorter duration.

This lovely Ruth, the mistress of the little habitation that now contains me, whom, at the moment when I despaired of knowing her, chance has so happily brought in my way, is all that her fine eyes express her to be – open, generous, sensible, and refined – uncultivated by art; but what has not nature bestowed upon her? Though my aunt has more than once chid me for the expression, I will yet call that chance happy, which put me in a situation to contemplate the ingenuousness and sensibility I was born to admire. Are the pains of the body to be regarded when so greatly overbalanced by the pleasures of the mind? I would describe her person to you, since her soul speaks through it, but that I fear even you may think it is rather the painting of fancy than truth; for though I will own I have seen a thousand faces which have excelled hers in every thing but expression, yet her eyes I never saw equalled – they are mild, blue, and intelligent; and when she raises them from some object beneath to look at your face, there is a winning softness in them that passes description. Surely to behold them without forming an exalted opinion of her soul, is impossible. I have read, or rather I have repeated Werter to her: I knew she would admire it. I shall soon quit my chamber, when I am to be introduced to her Frank; and will now relate to you the little history Mrs. Aylesby has given me of herself. –

'Such as you this day see me,' said she, whilst a blush crimsoned her cheeks, 'I am the daughter of a clergyman, and, I will not attempt to conceal it from you, a man not more worthy than he was necessitous. When I was but eleven years old, I lost that tender father, whom I yet remember with a soft regret which I am persuaded you can conceive, and which still continues to endear him to me. When I saw the grave which received those dear remains, and beheld it cover him for ever, child as I was, I believed myself incapable of surviving; but I have lived to lose the mother, by whose side I then wept, so equally tender and so equally beloved – I saw her ashes mingled with those of a husband but too dear. The cold sod which concealed them from my eyes, congealed for ever those channels through which the soft consciousness of filial affection had been so long accustomed to flow – they were closed never more to be opened.'

Ruth stopped to weep at the remembrance; and you, my brother, who know the tears which I have shed for that dear and amiable woman, who, in the being she gave to me, resigned her own into the hands of her Creator[26], will conceive how much I was affected. My heart, which has so often and so eagerly panted to pour itself out at the feet of that other dear, though deluded parent, how was it oppressed! But I will not remove the veil you have so tenderly endeavoured to throw over his foibles. Surely she, whom my father once made his wife, injured as I was by her artifice, must be secure: her name shall not be mentioned by me with detestation.[27] – Alas! who can be proof against the deceptions of those they love?

Involuntarily I joined my tears with those of Ruth, and mourned with her over a path of happiness which had never been opened to me, and recalled those ideas which from infancy had been used to agitate me. She saw my emotion, stopped and hesitated. I entreated her to proceed. She stifled her sighs – she dispersed the tears from her own eyes, fearful of wounding me. I saw her attention, and it was not for me to be insensible to it. From that moment my soul flew out to meet, it seemed capable of mingling with hers. – Mrs. Aylesby continued her narration.

'A few months before my losing that dear mother, she had bestowed me on a worthy man. Perhaps, had I chosen for myself – '

Ruth blushed, and again hesitated; but I looked down, and she continued –

'The importunities of such a mother, it had been ingratitude and impiety to refuse. Mr. Aylesby loved me; he had an excellent heart, and was possessed of a decent competency. I ought to have been happy – and I was happy with him; for I was convinced the last moments of that dear woman were rendered more easy by the protection she had procured for her daughter. It was the soft sigh of placid resignation that she breathed in my bosom – that last, that lamented one, in which her unpolluted soul escaped from mortality. I have sat on her grave at the grey twilight of evening – I have visited it with the first beams of the morning; and on the turf which concealed her, all the flowers of the spring have been taught to blossom. Shall I confess my weakness to you, Miss Morven? It was a blow I had not prepared myself for – I was married, yet she it was who was most dear to me, and for a short time my reason, too feeble to suppress, became a martyr to my feelings. It was to the care and tenderness of the worthy man whom she had confided me to, that I owe perhaps its restoration. After that period, a few months only had passed in which I had been able to testify my gratitude to him, before he was himself seized with a fever, which on the ninth day robbed me of the greatest support I had experienced. My little Sophy, whom I baptised after her grandmother, was then an infant. His small estate died with him, (being settled on his nephew,) and the pittance which the law then afforded me, with some little works of my own, have since supported myself and the dear little one in the manner which you now see.'[28]

She stopped, and I thanked her a thousand times for her condescension; but I will own to you I was not contented. Who was this Frank whom I had first seen? Frank I had heard her call him. I asked her with some hesitation, she answered with greater, but at last, with that sweet ingenuousness of manner which had won me to her, 'I will own,' said she, 'before I was ever engaged to Mr. Aylesby, I had seen another – this Frank – he is a distant relation – in short, might I have chosen for myself, it had been him: but he had quitted the village where I then resided, and I could not dream that he had thought of me. My dear mother believed Mr. Aylesby could make me happy. I was united to him, and never during his life did I see this young man; and for three years which I have passed in widowhood, he has been on a voyage to China. I had almost forgotten that he existed; at least I flattered myself I had: but a few days ago I was surprised with the sight of him, and fainted before he could speak; and that day, Miss Morven, on which I first saw you, – how doubly dear will it ever be to my heart! – was that on which my Frank first made an avowal of affection to me – Could I do otherwise than believe him? – '

She concluded, vainly endeavouring to hide her blushes. I wanted words to express how much she had obliged me; but her eyes could understand me without; they expressed to her how much her charming candour and tenderness have enchanted me. – I shall soon be introduced to this Frank, whom it is easy to see she loves; and I, my dear brother, was born, I believe, to love nothing equal to you.

LETTER XII.

I HAVE seen and conversed with Frank, but know not how it is, I am not yet of intelligence with him – I do not, in fact, find him all that I expected. His eyes dark, bright, and penetrating, there is soul in them; but are they those of a lover? Do they follow incessantly the mild expression of my Ruth's, of his Ruth's? Does he not rather receive than return the affection which glows on her cheek, and the tenderness that trembles on her lip? He is capable of talking to a stranger of graces, of other graces than those of his lovely widow. – I already dislike him; for he seems unworthy of the affection she bears him, and I could almost think insensible to it. He can fix his looks on another, and even distresses me with his attention. How shall I despise this Frank, whom I expected to admire, if he is capable of playing with her tenderness!

I am new to the world, yet already, my brother, have I observed that cruel serenity with which your sex can behold the embarrassment of ours. Boldly they fix their eyes on us – we are covered with confusion, and wish to shrink into ourselves; but that gaze, so distressing, pursues us, and the language of our blushes is not understood. You accuse us of vanity, and peruse us with a scrutinizing eye, as if willing to mortify us. It is not beauty alone which attracts those looks so perplexing: there is no face but has been sometimes so perused, and for what, but to add to the too visible uneasiness already glowing there? My imagination is raised by this conduct. Once, I remember, it conquered me. In a room full of company, at Lady Carlton's, a young man, for near an hour, had fixed his eyes on me; at last he came behind, and, resting on my chair, seemed as if willing to penetrate my heart through the light covering that concealed it. I could almost have wished that the glance which I gave him as I quitted the room with precipitation had been mortal. When I met him once afterwards, he offered an apology, and was more disgusting to me than ever. – But to my present situation.

I have made up a little library here, in a closet which joins to the room I am now in, and when I go I shall even leave my Werter with this Ruth, who has already attached me: and to the dear girl, whom she has taught already to read, I have given the works of the charming Countess of Genlis[29], those works so formed to open the heart, and awaken it to all the finer sensations. You will scarce believe how much I envy to France the birth of that benevolent writer. I find with pleasure Sophy already comprehend something of her story of Pamela.[30] Those pleasing and animating pictures of the infant heart, when shall I say to myself I have sufficiently perused them?

With what pleasure do I place the flowers which Sophy gathers from the fields for me next my heart? – I have walked out to the village more than once, and find that my aunt and I are much talked of there, a whisper being circulated that we are certainly somebody. A lover would surely take that opportunity of staying with his mistress; but, on the contrary, Frank accompanies, and is attentive to us, and I like him less than ever.

LETTER XIII.

IT is Sunday, and I went this morning to church. How shall I express to you the surprize or the rapture I there experienced! You should imagine a man, who has been blind from his birth, in one moment blest with universal vision and unbounded intelligence – you should think in what sounds he would express himself, with all the mercies of heaven, all the beauties of nature, pouring in upon him at once; and perhaps, my brother, you might then form some idea of the manner in which I have this day heard the Benedicite read.[31] Surprized, I fixed my eyes on the reverend deliverer. The curate of a neglected country village fulfilled to my soul all that it ever imagined of energy, propriety, sublimity, and feeling. The notes from an organ, full, clear, melodious, modulated, are nothing to his voice; since the animated expression – that expression, the offspring only of the human heart – informs every inflection of it, and every sound seems only to pass through his lips but to owe its origin to the soul. –

I was greatly flattered by his finding something in me worthy of his attention. I thought I more than once caught his eye, and, when the service was ended, was honoured by his requesting me to sit this afternoon in his pew; and at the same time, with an air of kind prepossession, he invited me to drink tea with his wife. I own I long to enter into a conversation with him, of which I almost feel myself unworthy. You will believe that the man who thus read the Benedicite, performed all other parts of the service equally devoutly, equally wonderfully. Ruth will not accompany me; and when I told her the pleasure which I promised myself, she smiled. Could I believe it possible for her to smile satirically, I should have been alarmed for this new favourite – but no, I will rather believe it to be at that warmth with which I already interest myself concerning him.

I have since walked out with Sophy: to hear the prattle of the innocent, to gather the sentiments of their hearts, to see the little eyes glisten when you talk of the necessity of leaving them, and to listen to those enchanting expressions of affection which we know to be sincere; is there a pleasure on earth to compare with it?

I like Mrs. Aylesby's lover better than I did: he did not this morning offer to accompany me. When I came home, I found him sitting beside Ruth; her hand was in his, and his eyes seemed overflowing with tenderness. His soul may be more capacious than I have yet been able to conceive; he may be capable of loving with all the ardor this sweet woman deserves; and he may yet be capable of paying me those attentions he may fancy I expect. He does not yet know me; if he did, he would be assured, that when his eyes assiduously follow her, when he forgets to give me the tea which she has just put in his hand, I think better of him than if he spent an hour in encomiums on myself.

LETTER XIV.

AH! my dear brother, the dews of the morning are not more rapidly dispelled by the beams of the summer sun, than the opinions I had formed have disappeared before conviction. The enthusiasm I boast of deceives me. The deception is removed, but the discovery that it was such has left a wound, and that the deepest, behind. The torrent of eloquence and energy which I had heard, flung a mist before my eyes: he who had enchanted me with it, seemed struck with the sensibility I could not repress, and I was blinded compleatly.

I have been again to church; I have passed two hours in the company of this wonderful reader, this enchanting preacher, and I have not another favourable epithet to add. – But I should tell you what has disgusted me: read on, and you will own I have reason to be so.

I accepted the curate's invitation, and accompanied him home. Ever desirous of expressing myself rather with energy than volubility, I was now more than usually silent. He gave me the characters of several of his parishioners as they passed, and I was sorry to find them, by his description, so little worthy of their pastor. I observed the poignancy of his wit; I could not avoid also observing the severity of his satire. When arrived at his house, I was received there by his wife; the ease of whose manners would grace a duchess, and the motherly affection with which she seemed to view me, won her my whole heart.

This couple have one son, the object in which their mutual affections seem to centre. He is the last of many children. My heart bled when I beheld this dear and only hope oppressed with sickness, and only kept by continual attention, as Ruth had before informed me, from the grave. I witnessed with sympathising pity the apprehensive tenderness which breathed through every accent of the trembling parents. I was really struck with them, they seemed no less so with me; and I will own that the compliments I received from both, though too pointed wholly to agree with my ideas of delicacy, were yet very grateful to me – to my vanity perhaps I should say. A thousand enquiries – how shall I say it? – a thousand impertinent enquiries succeeded – my income, my family, where I was going, on what account – in short, all that the most insatiable curiosity could suggest, or all that a mind the most unfeeling and unpolished could demand. Embarrassed and confused at the gross improprieties I found this person, who had so charmed me, to be capable of, I wished only to escape. I stayed, however, long enough to see him guilty of worse than flagrant unpoliteness and mean curiosity.

A young man rode up to the gate on horseback – You shall hear the character the curate gave him, and I will, if possible, have patience to tell you what passed afterwards. 'That,' said he, 'is the son of a neighbouring gentleman: you see in him, my dear child, one of the most profligate and despicable young fellows breathing.' He on whom this character was bestowed, alighted, however, and when he entered, believe me, I do not exaggerate, the same look of cordiality and appearance of pleasure I had been flattered by, were resumed. Mr. Manville the curate, even expressed a regard for the young man, whom a minute before he had represented as despicable and profligate, pressed him to stay with all the apparent earnestness of friendship, and engaged him for some weeks next shooting season.

I was totally confounded. Grieved and indignant, I did not even trust my eyes. Mr. Manville introduced me to this stranger. You will not wonder that I have not terms to express my detestation, when I tell you, that this reverend monitor was capable of raising a blush on the cheek of modesty: in short, he forgot he was a gentleman, and took pleasure in the bold laugh which he gave rise to in the young man, and the confusion with which he covered me. – Think what I felt in discovering that indelicacy is a term of praise to what he deserves. – I quitted him with precipitation, and the hand which I had before given him as a father, almost as a saint, shrunk from his. Cold and disgusted as I was, his penetrating eye and smiling countenance perused mine. If unconquerable and undisguised contempt was written there, can I help it? I am not formed to dissemble.

On my return, I wept in the bosom of the gentle Ruth – she knew him. Alas! his life is marked with duplicity; – yet she knows him capable of benevolent actions. My aunt chid me. 'It is this,' said she, 'I blame in you: – a man has talents; he has some of the virtues, and you expect him to be possessed of all. You dream, my child; awaken yourself, or the shocks you must yet have to suffer, will overcome you. A little less ardor and more moderation in your expectations had secured you from this. I can detest his faults, and may be perhaps even surprised at, but I am not overcome by them.' – My aunt may be right; I will believe she is; but, ah! my dear brother, she verges on fifty, and I, as to the world, am but an infant.

On Tuesday I quit this dear asylum and its benevolent mistress. She sighs at the approaching separation; but when I am gone, her Frank will be every thing to her.

To-morrow is the first day of May, and I have prepared some rustic decorations. Perhaps I may tell you of them.

My aunt has been more impatient than myself at this delay – she rallies me on the regard I feel for Ruth, and is surprized, she tells me, that I, who behold talents and genius with such admiration, and with all the envy which a heart not ignoble can entertain, should be attached to this soft and amiable being. – Ah! my brother, what has genius, what have talents to do with the affections? We may admire the understanding, but it is the heart only we love. In Ruth I find all the simple and unaffected graces of nature. Perhaps I would travel miles to behold a Gibbon[32] or a Hayley[33], to view the features of a Reynolds[34] or a Copley[35]; and I should feel that gratification in seeing them, which the presence of a superior being might be supposed to produce; but for the soft intercourse of mutual friendship, we do not require to be dazzled only; it is sufficient that our hearts are moved, and we find ourselves pleased.

LETTER XV.

I FEEL my mind at this minute in a state of perplexity; for suspicions have arisen in it, which, if just, may be dangerous to the peace of my friend, to the quiet of my own heart – which, if unjust, I ought bitterly to reproach myself with. – You will smile perhaps when I tell you the trifle which has given rise to them.

Ruth and I this morning rose early, and strolled out to enjoy the fragrance which breathes from every shrub and flower, which the hand of nature scatters with wild and beautiful profusion on the earth. We had not proceeded far before Frank followed and overtook us. My eyes fixed in admiring the beauties which surrounded me, my heart in silently adoring their Almighty Creator, I did not at first perceive the cold and formal silence which he kept. I walked slowly forward, and, leaning on the first stile that presented itself, looked toward heaven, and lost all ideas but those of devotion: – but the approach of some labourers soon roused me, when removing a few steps to give way to them, I was surprized to see Frank looking in my face with an attention that confused me, whilst Ruth leaned on his arm, and was perusing his with no less. As I turned, Frank started, and held out his hand to offer me assistance I was not in need of, and then pressing his hat lower on his forehead, hemmed two or three times as if willing to speak, whilst the deepest crimson covered his whole countenance. Both Ruth and myself caught the glow which we could not help observing, and we all fixed our eyes on the ground, and proceeded for some minutes without uttering a syllable.

Perhaps I had not so much remarked this little occurrence, but for some words which yesterday struck me as they escaped Frank. He was with Ruth and myself, who were talking of Werter. He had sate silent for more than half an hour, till on Ruth's saying there could certainly be no misery equal to that of injuring the peace of those we love – not even that of loving ourselves without hope, – he started up, and catching Ruth's hand, who sate next him, said, with emotion – 'True, my dear Ruth, and when both those evils fall on one man, surely they should produce distraction.' – The sudden and earnest address startled her – He saw it, and seemed to endeavour at an air of tranquillity. – I had myself observed the vehemence with which he had expressed himself, and was happy that the entrance of my aunt gave a new turn to the conversation. – Frank, I know not why, was never a favourite of hers, and I could almost fancy he has seen it, and assiduously avoids intruding on her. – He soon after quitted the room, and the impression which the whole circumstance then made on my mind had worn off, but for that of this morning, which, trifling as it was, recalled and strengthened some fears which my own observation and some hints of my aunt had given rise to.

Our departure from hence is fixed for to-morrow, and perhaps I ought rather to rejoice at, than regret it.

* * *

Since I quitted my pen I have been much surprized. I will tell you things as they happened.

I had had a may-pole raised[36] – At noon all the children of the village assembled round it, their mothers bringing baskets of flowers – six of the prettiest (Sophy was one), in light running dresses, drawn round the bosoms, and tied trouser-wise at the little ankles, with a girdle of ribbon round their waist, stood expecting the signal for the race which I had appointed. The swiftest was to be queen, and I had prepared a garland to crown her.[37] I will own we thought our Sophy would win, and she was, as we expected, just at the pole, her little hands stretched forward to grasp it, when the child next to her fell down – she turned to assist her – another passed by, and claimed the prize – Poor Sophy burst into tears – I had been touched with the child's tenderness; for through that only she had forfeited the reward of victory. However, to be strictly impartial, I made another garland with some artificial flowers and pink ribbon, which happily her little rival preferred; and the wreath I had made for Sophy, of the only roses I had been able to procure, a sprig of myrtle[38], and here and there a white narcissus[39], fastened behind with a sky-blue ribbon, admirably suiting her fair hair, was adjusted to her head; but on the rest looking a little jealous, Ruth and I seated ourselves on the grass in the midst of them, and with a few cowslips[40] and violets[41] set all to rights, and, after a distribution of cakes and sweetmeats[42], they ran to form a ring round the may-pole. – I had thought it ill fixed in the morning; the wind rose a little, and I saw it was near falling. I screamed to the children, and flew myself forwards to support it; but, before I could reach it, I found myself drawn back, and (judge my surprize) I saw Burell dart before me, and avert the danger. The inclosure we were in was behind the house, and whilst my aunt was seated at one of the back windows, Burell had arrived, and had scarce spent a minute in enquiry.

When he saw the situation I had put myself in – it was dangerous enough, considering my but ill-recovered arm – he feared for me, and the rest happened as I told you.

Unable to account for his interposition, Ruth looked at me, and my wonder almost equalled her own; but Burell leaving the pole to the care of the country-folks, I gave him my hand – he is your friend, he must be mine. – His eyes sparkled with pleasure. 'Good God!' said he, trembling as he held it, 'what have I endured for these few days past! Is there a power on earth which can again oblige me to lose sight of you, even for a moment?'

His energy, his eyes fixed on my face, disconcerted me; I saw again the look of dejection I have before mentioned to you: I half withdrew my hand. 'Charming woman!' said he, as hesitating he detained it, 'what have I uttered? I had lost you – I am again at your side – can you expect me to be reasonable?'

At this minute Frank approached from the house, as if intending to join us; but scarce stopping, made a slight inclination to Burell; and quickening his pace, he passed on, and I have not since seen him. Burell's eyes followed him with a kind of stern curiosity, and when he had lost sight of him, he for the first time addressed himself to Ruth with an enquiry after Frank – an incoherent one, and surely it was needless. Her blushes might have told him who he was, and what he was to her.

The arrival of the stranger had disconcerted the whole group of little ones; to relieve them therefore, and desirous of knowing what had brought Burell on so sudden a visit, I led the way in, but could scarcely persuade Ruth to join us – she for the first time talked of intruding. In short, Burell's behaviour, and her looks, more archly intelligent than I had before seen them, have opened my eyes – or am I again deceiving myself?

When we joined my aunt, Burell told me, that when he last quitted us, he proceeded to Bath. – I am mistaken, if by his saying it my aunt gained any information. – When he found we did not arrive there, and when at last returning by the route he knew we should take, he could gain no intelligence of us, he was uneasy, to use his own words – he was frantic with apprehension. Night and day he travelled the road, till, after having discovered the stage we last quitted, and wandering near it yet in uncertainty, he met our servant in the village, who informed him of the place of our residence, and the accident which had detained us here.

This ardor, my dear brother, so like my own, and this attention to me, does it proceed from his friendship for you, and from the interest he takes in me as your sister only? I would willingly yet believe it possible from my own heart – I will believe it; for what is there, my brother, that, as your friend, I would not do for him?

The curate called in here this evening: he had heard of our intended departure, and could not, he said, deny himself the pleasure of spending half an hour in our company. The young man I mentioned before – you remember his opinion of him – was on his arm; could Mr. Manville then think to gratify me by that flattering language, that look of affection with which he addressed me? Is it possible, that, possessed of such talents himself, he imagines the rest of the world can neither compare nor combine? That vanity must indeed be egregious, which could be deceived by so flimsy a covering. Can the man, who, conversing with you, treats indiscriminately with contempt and degradation all who are mentioned, be weak enough to suppose you can think yourself exempted from his satire any longer than whilst you are with him? And whilst he seemed even to wish that I should observe the ironical compliments he paid this young man, could he suppose I was not conscious his treatment of me might be the same? He has the secret of adapting the deception to the object, and his mean soul can triumph in it. He now triumphs in it; but will the moment never be at hand when he shall wish, but in vain, to be disguised to himself – when those words of praise to a virtue unknown to him, "Behold an Israelite in whom there is no guile!"[43] like the voice of thunder, shall fall on his soul? Will the time never come, when, as a reproach he shall feel them, and shall envy the simplest son of nature to whom they can be applied?

LETTER XVI.

I HAVE quitted my amiable hostess. I do not know how it was, though I would have given the world to be without them, I felt a thousand forebodings – I strained her to my heart – it seemed ready to burst its prison – I looked at her sleeping Sophy, whom I had the courage not to awaken: one little hand was under her head, her fair locks curling round her delicate face: the flowers of yesterday were on her pillow. Lovely human blossom! and thou also must fade: said I to myself, as my tears fell on her forehead – She started and I hurried away. I asked for Frank; but late last night he took his horse, and left an apology with his Ruth – some sudden business he talked of – but when she told me of it, a sweet sadness sat on every feature. – My mind seemed strongly to forebode some misfortunes to one or both of them; but I would avoid these fancies, and I made Ruth promise to write to me.

When the chaise drove from her door, as she stooped over the little gate, when I saw the last waving of her handkerchief, my voice died on my lips. 'Tis true that when the fault was past repairing, I was angry with myself for the weakness I had shewn, and my aunt too seemed vexed. 'If your heart flies out thus to every stranger,' said she, 'what, my dear niece, will your existence be? If you feel so much in leaving an acquaintance of a week or two, how do you think the great misfortunes of life are to be borne?'

My aunt was perfectly right, and these were the very sentiments which had just passed in my own mind; yet I don't know how it was, her delivering them, and that with a little severity of tone too, recalled the very ideas she wished to destroy, and I was as weak again as ever. I attempted in vain to anticipate the pleasure I should experience in meeting with Ruth, and in seeing the improvement of her lovely infant. I know not why, but I felt my fears so much stronger than my hopes that I could scarce refrain from fresh tears: but I remembered my obligations to my aunt; her displeasure, I know, was mixed with uneasiness; they both arose only from her tenderness to me, and are equally calls on me to exert myself. I obeyed them; I appeared calm; and soon became more chearful.

LETTER XVII.

LIKE a stream stopped in its channel, this impetuous desire, which has lain awhile so still, returns with redoubled force. I read Werter again; I contemplate its beauties; I look forward to meeting with its author.

I scarce perceived till to-day that Burell again accompanies us. I am convinced, my dear brother, I think I may say convinced, that he loves me. I can say this to you without fearing that you should attribute it to vanity: – I have just found it out, and now wonder I have been so long blind. My aunt encourages his passion, which I own makes me uneasy. Perhaps he has told you of this unhappy partiality. I am sure I have not deserved it of him. I can respect him; I can wish him happy with another; but my heart, I am convinced, cannot answer to his. As to love, I can talk of it to you. If ever I shall feel that passion, it will like lightning penetrate my heart, and I fear it will in a moment be fixed there. I can see this is very unreasonable, but it is me. – Burell is a good creature; he can bear with, he can humour my foibles; but to be loved, he must sympathize with them: for that passion, so ardent, so unbounded, and when real so disinterested, I admire, but I acknowledge that I dread it – And you, my dear brother, have you no mistress but glory?

LETTER XVIII.

WE are now at Bath, where we arrived this evening. Burell had ridden forward to see that no accommodations were wanting for us, and I took that opportunity of speaking to my aunt, and of telling her what my sentiments of him are, and what they ever must be. She seemed both surprized and angry. Shall I say it, she was even severe – she called me whimsical and ungrateful. I bore it – I am bound to bear it from her; but do I deserve those epithets? Surely not, my brother. They sunk very deep into my heart.

In the fervor of my soul, I talked too of the project she had indulged me in, and again anticipated my pleasure and my triumph over those who mistake Werter, and see no moral in it. She answered me only with coldly saying, she thought I had grown wiser. I was silent; but since I parted with you, I have not felt such pain as the whole of her behaviour, cold, severe, and distant, gave me. She seems to think there may be another way of controlling me beside tenderness. – Never, my brother, will I forget the favours I receive; and as to injuries, I can forgive, but I am not insensible to them.

LETTER XIX.

My dear Brother,

I WILL own I am too impatient of control. My spirits were sinking, and what a cordial have I received! – I have received a letter from you, who have given me every thing, and who are every thing to me – from you, who excel me so much, and who can yet sympathize in all my feelings. You can allow the motives of them to be worthy, perhaps noble – but I see you think me extravagant. This passion for genius, has it found no visible object? you ask me; and shall I say it distressed me that you too mention Burell?

You send me the portrait of a lady, and ask my opinion of it: I will tell it you frankly. Shall I not say every thing, when I acknowledge your own cannot exceed it, and I can fancy I behold in the face all I think you worthy of, and all I think worthy of you? You know my heart, my dear brother, you will judge how perfect I then believe the mind which illuminates it.

I wish you was with me; for I have gained nothing by my journey. I find no road of enquiry open; my soul sickens at my disappointment. Like an eagle confined by a chain, who wishes in vain to soar to the gates of the morning, and behold the fountain of light, I am bound in the trammels of custom.

My aunt is more serious than ever; she perfectly shocks me. A young woman, she says, wanders about to search after a man. – She was not always so severe. Has she altered her opinion, or is it possible she before meant to deceive me?

Burell too persists almost ungenerously. – If my ideas and my affections are to be confined, I will quit them, I will quit England, and fly from their persecutions. The ardor of my soul is not, I cannot wish it to be subdued. They attempt to stop this torrent; but they mistake, they only encrease its rapidity.

LETTER XX.

FREDERICK BURELL *to Major* MORVEN.

Dear Morven,

WHEN first I acknowledged that passion for your sister, which I thought myself bound in honor to avow to you, I believed it incapable of increase; but I find every moment which has added to my knowledge of her virtues, has insensibly added also to my love for her. – I have been happy enough to render myself agreeable to your aunt; but your sister, whom I now believe above affectation, treats me with a marked reserve, which almost destroys my hopes, and with them my happiness.

I had flattered myself too much from the friendship with which she had honored me: from continually seeing her, she was become necessary to my peace, and I had cherished I know not what fancy, that time might make me so to hers. Whilst she remained in reality blind to my affection, a thought sometimes arose in my mind, that she was yet a woman, and might only appear to be so. I saw not, that, open and ingenuous as she is, she was incapable of the little artifices her sex are sometimes charged with; but, Morven, I have found, though too late, that, while she is every thing to me, I am to her nothing more than her brother's friend. But she is disengaged, and whilst she remains so, I will not yet despair – To resist unremitted perseverance is the province of few, and perhaps even her heart is capable of being subdued by it.

She has told you on what idea she came to Bath, and I now write to inform you of a scheme which I have formed in consequence of the end which she proposes in this journey. – She expects here to meet with the author of Werter: I believe that to be impossible; but a circumstance having happened which hastens my brother's departure from France, offering to me one on whose honor I can rely to personate this author, has given me the idea of engaging him so to do. Though I believe myself as jealous as even you can be in whatever relates to the delicacy of your sister, I would not go so far without informing you of it. I will relate to you, in a few words, the occasion of my brother's quitting Paris so soon, which did not a little surprize me, and you will recognize in it that impetuosity of temper which has ever characterized him.

At Versailles he became acquainted with a Madame le Mer, a widow lady of family, whose only daughter was long addressed by a young nobleman, to whom her affections were engaged. Madame le Mer went as usual to pass a month in the summer with her daughter, at a retired seat she possessed about a league from Versailles[44], during which time the lover paid them no further visits. Vincent, who had been invited by Madame le Mer to spend the week with them in their retirement, saw the grief of the young lady, and was informed of the source of it by her mother. As hasty in executing as he is quick in conceiving an idea, he set out unsolicited for Paris, where the lover resided, designing to enter into an explanation with him. On arriving at his house, Vincent immediately desired to be introduced to him; but was surprized with an account of his being on the point of marriage with another lady, with whom he was at that time gone on a little excursion. He enquired the route they had taken, followed, and overtook them, who were then in fact on their way to be married; and had been joined just without the town by a grand cavalcade[45], consisting mostly of the relations of the intended bride. Without debating a moment, Vincent, approaching the carriage, where he discovered the unfaithful lover and his intended lady, ordered it to stop.

He then told his name and business, and insisted on the nobleman's alighting. The young man, though confounded at this address, ordered the coach to proceed, saying it was only a mad-headed Englishman; but Vincent leaped from his horse, and in a moment opened the coach door, and handed the gentleman into the road, and without much ceremony insisted on his immediately defending himself, or mounting the horse he had just quitted, and returning immediately to Mademoiselle le Mer. Enraged, he chose the latter alternative, and Vincent, entering the carriage, applied himself to consoling the lady the intended bridegroom had just quitted, and to her family, who highly incensed gathered round him, he explained the whole motives of his actions, at the same time declaring himself ready to meet any one who thought they had a right either to question or blame him. The lady, however, acknowledging herself satisfied, nothing further arose; but the affair made so much noise that Vincent wished to escape from a place where he had rendered himself remarkable. He received the thanks of Madame le Mer, whose daughter was weak enough to pardon her lover, and to be married to him in a short time afterwards.

Vincent has also, I understand, from another quarter, an additional motive for quitting Paris; the friends of the lady having given him hints of a passion with which his gallantry has inspired her. Be that as it will, I know his aversion to being shewn and complimented, and therefore expect him over soon. – If you should not disapprove the idea I have thrown out, I shall certainly pursue it.

I was happy to meet, some time since, with colonel Bolton, who had then just returned from Gibraltar; but the account I heard from him of you, gave me an uneasiness which I was unable to conceal from the penetrating eye of your sister, and when she then enquired after you, I answered her rather consonant to my hopes than my wishes.

Adieu, dear Morven! I will guard your secret, but I should be very unhappy, if you concealed any material alteration from your friend. – Write to me soon and sincerely, and believe me to remain, with unalterable affection and friendship,

Yours,
FREDERICK BURELL.

LETTER XXI.

MY aunt is certainly right, my dear brother, when she tells me that slight incidents affect me too much. Why is it then, that with all the pain which this disposition causes me, I wish not to be other than I am? They would persuade me – my aunt and Burell I mean – that I am very ill; and, to oblige them, or, to speak more justly, to avoid their importunities, I have confined myself to my chamber.

What is the world to me, if I am not permitted to roam in it as I please, to seek out those with whom my soul is in unison? I declare to you, whom I know capable of believing me, that all which it contains is tedious and even disgusting to me, otherwise than as it moves the mind and its affection – in short, otherwise than as it relates to the heart.

I travelled here under a false hope; I see it disappointed, perhaps even derided; and the city which I am now in, seems a boundary scarce less narrow to me than the dungeon of a criminal, who, at the expected moment of escaping from darkness and doubt, finds the door which confines him still guarded without intermission and without pity.

At my aunt's request, I have attended her to drink the waters. On casting my eyes round the scene of sickness which presented itself, new to a sight so distressing, you will easily judge the feelings which it excited. I beheld, painted in all the warm and glowing colours of imagination, the mothers who should so soon weep over the ashes of their children – the children who should water the grave of their parents with tears. Melted as I felt myself, I was yet capable of concealing those emotions, when I perceived a young soldier, who pressed near me; pale, wan, emaciated, he seemed scarce hovering on the last verge of existence. With a trembling hand, a neat young woman, who accompanied him, presented the glass to him – it was his sister. I have no words to explain the anguish which I felt at my heart; but you can conceive, my dear brother, and can account for it. Fool that I was, the glass dropped from my hand, and I seemed surrounded by darkness and confusion. On my recovery, the attention I had excited covered me with blushes. As I rose to come away the eyes of the whole room followed me, and the murmur of enquiry and pity reached my ears. When seated in the carriage, I first took notice of an elegant young man who had assisted in supporting me to it, and recovered myself sufficiently to join in my aunt's compliments to him for the assistance which he had offered me. She could not deny the permission he requested to wait on her, of which he has already availed himself; and I am happy to have had an opportunity of acquitting myself toward him with more propriety than was before in my power. Burell was present; his visits to my aunt, or rather to me, though I receive them not as such, are as constant as ever: I have by chance heard an opinion of his; assiduity, he told my aunt, would gain any woman, and she seemed to join with him; but he deceives himself, my dear brother: though without it we are not to be won, he will find that neither are we always gained with it. Persuasion may subdue a weak, pity a too gentle mind; but his rule will not then be universal.

Burell, though I think with haughtiness, returned his thanks also to my aunt's new visitor; and, when he quitted us, informed us how necessary it was to be careful of what acquaintance we cultivated here: but his good humour did not seem much encreased, when my aunt told him, by the enquiries she had thought proper to make, she knew this young man to be the only son of Lord S——, who had been ordered to Bath for the recovery of his health – though perhaps more to pacify his father, who had been lately reduced almost to despair by a slight illness of his.

This conversation dropped, and Burell then joined my aunt in urging me to submit to have some advice, and in telling me that slight incidents, as I have before said, made too strong an impression on my mind. I know my dear aunt's tenderness for me; and, though not at all convinced by her arguments, I have submitted to her wishes, and the physician has felt my pulse, shakes his head, and advised some days of tranquillity and retirement. As to retirement, I acquiesce; but whilst my mind remains agitated by wishes unfulfilled, and hopes, though clouded, unsubdued, I shall have little to do with tranquillity.

LETTER XXII.

I AM convinced, that, in half the sickness of the world, it is the mind which should be consulted more than the frame.

My aunt has told the physician, whom she obliges to attend me, the warmth and impetuosity, the peculiarity, as she calls it, of my disposition. She wished him to deny me the enjoyment of those moments when time so rapidly flies, those hours which I delight to spend in reading, or in writing to my dear brother; but he seems to understand me better, and they are again allowed me – for I have been for some days denied them both. I have myself had some conversation with Dr. C—— and he does not seem to think of immuring me any longer. He is chearful, amiable, accessible, and has invited us to visit him. I heard him say something to my aunt of drawing my attention from those objects which at present engross it too much. 'Can there be no means,' he said, 'of satisfying this fancy of hers?' These expressions of his induce me to hope that I shall engage this good man in my cause. As to my illness, believe me, nothing but the tenderness of my aunt's fears can make her even imagine it dangerous.

I am more than half angry with Ruth; for she has not yet written to me. Her heart so warm to love, can it be cold, is it therefore insensible, to the duties of friendship? If it is so, am I not right, when I wish that this passion, which consumes all ties but its own, may remain still a stranger to my breast?

LETTER XXIII.

ACCORDING to Dr. C——'s advice, I go to the pump-room[46] now to drink the waters, though I cannot apprehend the benefit which will accrue to me from being every morning made sick. On my complaining, he has remedied this a little by leaving the quantity to my own judgment. There I regularly see the Mr. S—— whom I have mentioned to you, and who has since visited us. I find something of elegance and refinement about him, which I have not before met with. There is a soft politeness, an appearance even of tenderness in his compliments, which is very prepossessing. He saw my aunt frequently during my few days of confinement. This morning his father Lord S—— was in the room, whose eyes scarce a moment quitted this darling son, though he himself did not join our party, of which during our short stay his son made one.

The morning being damp, Burell almost forced my aunt to hurry away, fearful, he said, of my catching cold. Why will he interest himself thus about me, who am unworthy of his attachment, and who have sincerely and definitively told him the impossibility of my returning it? When I see how the coldness, so different to my nature, which I assume towards him, wounds and afflicts him, I am scarce capable of preserving it; yet he still obliges me to treat him otherwise than as a friend, since too plainly I perceive, when with confidence and tenderness I speak to him as such, he imagines I am become favourable to him as a lover. He forces me to think myself of this importance to him, and I therefore, for his sake, hear with pleasure that he intends absenting himself some time from us. He goes to meet a brother who has been abroad some years. Happy Burell! And if half my wishes were accomplished, never would he be otherwise – A heart open to the affections of nature cannot deserve to be miserable.

On my entering the pump-room this morning we were delayed a few minutes by the press, when, on turning to receive the apologies of some person who had a good deal incommoded me, the intelligent countenance of a lady, who stood near, interested me at the first glance. We were scarce entered before I perceived the universal attention which was attracted, and in a moment the name of *Lee* circulated in a whisper[47], which, with the look directed so near our party, and that had at first half distressed me, informed me of the object which had excited it. – And this then, thought I, is the *Temeraire*[48], whose name has been publicly joined with that of one of the first female writers of our age!

My prepossession for her vanished; since who, my dear brother, is there that should be ranked with the writer of Cecilia[49]? There is a strength of mind and nobleness of sentiment pervading that whole work, which has often forced tears from my eyes, and has warmed and enraptured my heart.

I wished, however, to address this celebrated author; but Mr. S—— joined us, and, before my attention was again disengaged, she was so much surrounded, I could not think of breaking through the circle she had attracted, and Burell, too anxious for my health, staid not till it was dispersed.

I will read this Recess[50], of which she is the author, if I shall be able to procure it; for so watchful is my aunt of my health, that all which could enlighten my mind she would deny as hurtful to my body. This body, my dear brother, this texture of dust and ashes, why are we so careful of preserving it? For my own part, I regard it only as the case of that invaluable essence, whose powers I believe it our duty to call forth, whose vigour we were born but to exercise.

LETTER XXIV.

BURELL has now quitted me, and set out to meet his brother. He entered just after our breakfast, and I was leaving the room to dedicate some hours to music. It is the science of the feeling soul, and was wont to chear me in the lone days of confinement and ignorance. He knows my arrangement, and I was retiring without apology, when in a low and hasty voice he recalled me. 'Forgive me, Theresa,' said he, 'I ask only a minute – one minute, the last perhaps on this subject.'

I heard his hesitation, his emotion, and how could I avoid returning? 'On all subjects,' said I, 'on any subject but one, I must hear with pleasure my brother's friend and mine.'

Why was he so agitated as I pronounced these words? Why did he faintly and inarticulately repeat – 'His friend and yours' – O! too dear and charming appellation! – O word, which from those lips informs me I must never hope to gain more! – Why is my soul wrung? – Why was I born not to be content with it?

He pressed his hand on his forehead – he looked steadfastly on me, and his agitation seemed to encrease.

My aunt had hastily left the room; I would have now given the world she had been near. I feared to encrease his emotion, already too painful; yet how could I act with tenderness to him, with justice to myself – I, who know his wishes, and my own heart, insensible as to them?

One moment I held out my hand to him, the next I feared his constructions, and hastily withdrew it. The motion, however, had not escaped him; with more composure than before, he held out his. 'I understand you, Theresa,' said he, melting into tears – 'as a friend only' – O treasure every way inestimable! – tender and invaluable pledge, I will endeavour to receive it as such.

He took my extended hand. – I feel, my dear brother, I yet feel the sorrow-ful and tender pressure with which he detained it in both his. – I had remained silent, fearing to add to his emotion by my own: my voice, had I before spoken, would have revealed it. When I again saw the increasing violence of his, I sum-moned my resolution to dispel it, and, making enquiries concerning his brother, I congratulated him on their expected meeting. I spoke of my happiness in you, my dear brother, and of the friendship you bear to him. He looked at me, but seemed almost insensible that I addressed him, till I talked of his quitting Bath. 'Yes, Theresa,' said he, 'charming Theresa! you are now my friend; you must then allow me to speak to you as such – and is there any term which can express how dear you are to me, how necessary the sight of you is almost to my existence?' – 'Of this friendship let us talk no more,' hastily said I – 'yours I cannot doubt, and if you will trust to mine, never, Burell, shall you be deceived in it.' – A doubt-ful pleasure seemed to gleam in his eyes as I spoke. – 'Trust to it,' repeated he – O if salvation depended on it! –

Too plainly I beheld in his countenance an emotion, the offspring of latent expectation, and again broke in upon him. 'You will, I am assured,' said I, 'believe that all which I profess I feel; and let me, Burell, conjure you, painful though necessary task, let me conjure you to believe also, that all which I feel I have pro-fessed.' – 'It is enough, Theresa,' his voice again faltering. 'One thing only I have to request of you as a friend: suffer me to devote myself to your welfare; as such, as that friend only I would ask. Forgive me, I have one wish' –

He hesitated, but he saw me attentive, and proceeded –

'O that as a friend I might be thought worthy of your confidence; and that when, in the days yet to come, you shall yield to another, when you shall bestow the heart I must now hope for no more – that heart whose emotions I have watched over and adored when present – whose lovely and beloved owner has alone occupied me when absent. – But, Theresa, I forget myself; yet when in some happier moment by another shall be gained that jewel, inestimable to me' –

The trembling agitation with which he spoke, pained me; I thought I under-stood him, and wished to spare us both a further explanation.

'Burell,' said I, 'it is a testimony of friendship which I owe you, and that moment, if ever it shall arrive, I promise to confide to you.' – 'Noble, amiable condescension,' said Burell; 'yet what is there I should be surprised at from you?'

I was willing to interrupt a conversation but too painful, and continued – 'I believe – I know you, Burell, to be too generous to make any use of it which could injure either the affections or the honour of Theresa. From me, Burell, believe me, you shall ever command all the effusions of gratitude, and all the warmth of esteem.'

I stopped, fearful of saying more. He read my uneasiness in my face, and pressing the hand I had again given him as a confirmation of my promise, he bent over it in silence, and then hastily quitted me. The best wishes of my heart went with him. The tears which I had restrained from flowing, now gave ease to my spirits, too apt to be oppressed. His look, as he left me, soft, tender, un-upbraiding, a thousand sentences had less affected me. You, my brother, knowing as you do every emotion of my soul, will not, I am sure, blame me. You may feel pity for your friend, but let not that pity overcome your love for your sister.

I will own my aunt's behaviour has surprized me; she seems to have ceased being his advocate, and has not even asked, since Burell this morning quitted me, the intent of his speaking to me, nor the end which it produced. But why should I wonder at her tenderness to me, of which she every day gives me new proofs?

We were to have gone to Dr. C——'s in the evening; but this day I dedicate to Burell: how many has he not bestowed upon me! I should be but too happy, might I hope never myself to want that pity which I now unaffectedly bestow on him.

LETTER XXV.

Mrs. Deborah Carlton *to Colonel* Morven.

My dear Nephew,

AFTER my having procured that justice to be done to your sister which you was so willing to complete, and having afterwards, at your request, taken her under my protection, I am convinced you can have no doubt of the sincerity of my affection to you both. – Whatever remonstrances, therefore, I shall lay before you concerning her, I am certain, with all your affection for her, you will receive and consider as you ought.

You must have observed from her letters, how every new emotion hurries her away: mild and gentle as she is in other things, when once some object for her impetuosity interposes, she is not to be withstood; she fixes her mind with a fantastical earnestness on one point, and then sees nothing with complacency, but what tends toward it. Who but herself ever thought of setting out in search of an author, because she is persuaded, she knows not why, that he is an Englishman, and fancies herself the only person in the world who does him justice.

The indifferent state of her health, which I see with a concern I cannot sufficiently express, inclined me to yield to the entreaties of your friend Mr. Burell: indeed, I could think of no other method to dissipate that unremitting attention she had, I fear, too long paid to her studies, than by seemingly giving into this whim of hers. To speak the truth, nephew, I know not what to do with one whom opposition afflicts and oppresses. After much deliberation and persuasion, I agreed, therefore, to this deception, hoping that in seeming to be fulfilled, her wishes would insensibly wear out; but the event has not answered my expectation, and the unfortunate overturning of our chaise, by the accident it occasioned to her, seemed to add another blow to her health, before but indifferently established.

Again too, at Mrs. Aylesby's, taken up with the friendship she formed with her, she was blind to a passion with which, evidently to me, she from the first moment inspired the lover of her new friend. She had before, when wholly occupied with her books, been no less so to that of Mr. Burell. If I had not myself hurried her away from this spot, I know not what confusion she might have been the cause of; I could not but dread the pain which a heart so generous as hers would have felt, had she staid to make the discovery. – As nothing, however, is more likely to stop a rising passion than a total insensibility to it in its object, I am in hopes this affair, which has given me some uneasiness, will go no further, and I shall find some excuse in our return to take another route than that which leads to Mrs. Aylesby.

She there also convinced me how happy it is for her, that she possesses that independence you so nobly settled on her. Though with five hundred pounds a year, she bestows as if she had five thousand.[51] Under the name of gratifications for the docility of the child, she introduced conveniences for her mother, and furnished out a wardrobe with less offence to the delicacy of the receiver, than a common person would have bestowed a trinket.

When we quitted Mrs. Aylesby's, though, by your friend Burell's following her there, her eyes were open to him, he gained nothing by it; nor did her former hopes of searching out and finding this author lose any thing by the delay. I was almost as much surprized as chagrined when I made this discovery, and I believe the manner in which I spoke to her informed her of it; but her mind is too fervent for the delicacy of her frame. The uncertain state I see her health in, subdues me when I wish to be most severe; and I find myself obliged to resume that gentleness which my judgment would bid me disallow.

Mr. Burell, who is but too anxious about her, ever since our arrival here, has been conjuring me to give way to another scheme, which, he thinks, by carrying the deception something further, more likely to satisfy her; and I have promised, after one more endeavour to wean her mind from this fancy, to consent to it.

The physician who attends her, interests himself much concerning her: I have told him her whim, and he has proposed to enter into the subject with her. But the principal end of my writing is to tell you I much wish you to be near her, since I know the power you have over her, and that what you disapprove, I am certain, she would at any time avoid.

Do not suffer yourself to be carried away in the same manner as herself, nor, through a romantic admiration of the general you have so well distinguished yourself under, suffer your sister to want that protection which her peculiar turn of mind, her inexperience, and her very attractive person, put her so much in need of. With a thousand graces, of which she is charmingly unconscious, she is now almost first entering into a world, where I plainly see she will not fail of engaging attention and admiration. To the striking advantages of height, grace, and complexion, she joins the most attractive manners and expressive countenance. I do not therefore wonder that she has already gained a lover here in the only son of a nobleman, a young man, worthy it should seem of the rank he is born to inherit. I see no reasonable objection, should any proposal on his part arise, and which I have little doubt but there will; yet she paid a thousand times more attention to the entrance of a young lady, who has lately distinguished herself as a writer, than to all the compliments of this new and elegant lover. For my part, nephew, I tremble lest some designing person should get scent of that peculiar turn of mind of hers, which might lay her open to arts of which she would be the last person in the world to imagine herself the object.

I hope what I have here said may be sufficient to incline you to hasten over, to be near to support and direct her: if it is not, what else can I say which may not too much alarm you?

When I first began my letter, I did not intend to mention to you what my fears tell me is perhaps too necessary. This dear, this amiable girl, how shall I write it to you? – I fear she has never perfectly recovered herself from that violent and malignant fever which she caught during her attendance on me. I watch her health, and have many reasons to fear its decline. The unremitting eagerness with which she has pursued after knowledge from the time of her being with me, has, I fear, impaired a constitution naturally delicate. In the first earnestness of enquiry she wished to comprehend every thing at once, and, all her talents being in their full perfection, the rapidity of her own progress, which surprized every tutor she employed, encouraged her, perhaps too much indeed, to persevere. Rest, food, pleasure, with her, all gave way to study. She must perceive an alteration in herself; yet her temper retains all its sweetness, and her mind all its gentleness as well as its force. If this should really be the case, if a slow and devouring disease, contracted in the kindest offices of grateful tenderness, is really consuming this dear and lovely girl, how can I support the thoughts of it?

Dr. C——, an eminent physician, who attends her here, tells me I am too apprehensive; but there is no making those gentlemen of the faculty explicit. He would have me introduce her into a larger circle than she has yet moved in, and, for this reason indeed principally, as he said, ordered her every morning to attend the pump-room; but there I see with pain one object of compassion engages her attention more strongly than all the giddy multitude with which she is surrounded, and distress reaches her susceptible and unexperienced heart, with a force which she can neither prevent nor conceal.

I will yet hope that I have been too apprehensive; I do not doubt, however, but that from the whole of what I have said, you will think it necessary to be near her: your presence every way may do much for her. In the mean time, be convinced of my tenderest care and affection for her; and be assured yourself, I shall ever remain,

Hers and your affectionate aunt,
D. CARLTON.

LETTER XXVI.

Miss MORVEN *to Colonel* MORVEN.

I HAVE had a dispute, my dear brother; I had almost said I had gained a victory for the author of Werter.

We went this afternoon to Dr. C——'s. In our way thither we were not a little frightened, and we were again obliged to Mr. S—— for his assistance; but how that happened I can tell you afterwards: as it was, we went in his carriage to Dr. C——'s, who introduced us to his daughter. She is a genteel young woman: she may have sense perhaps, but, by her silence concerning every thing but cards and fashions, I can be no judge of it.

Happily there was a party without me. My aunt and a brother of Dr. C——'s sat down to whist[52] with a gentleman and Miss C——. The doctor seated himself next me, and we entered into conversation, which he politely turned on books, those sources of knowledge and entertainment, those delightful improvers of the heart and understanding, in which we behold the manners of past ages, the heroes of other times. We read of the errors of man, and are humbled: we hear of the virtuous and the mighty, and emulation, the offspring of generous admiration, throbs through our hearts. How often have I wished that I were like them! How often to the dead, to the living, have I envied those deeds of glory, those works of genius, which it was theirs to perform, which it is mine only to admire!

I believe I express myself more warmly than the rest of the world; and when I would explain my sentiments, the impetuosity of them hurries me away. I cannot, my dear brother, mention the sons and daughters of fame without emotion. It was thus, that, in talking to Dr. C——, my own energy stopped me; I felt my eyes too near overflowing, and endeavoured to speak more calmly. He seemed to agree with my sentiments, and owned our obligations to the children of genius.

'But it is to those,' said he, 'who would point out the right path, to whom we are obliged – who would take us, as it were, by the hand, and, as they lead us in the flowery road of fable, would shew us the errors we should shun, and the guilt we must learn to avoid – to these my dear madam, we are obliged: but what shall we say to the man, who, under the mask of fable and fancy, would subvert every principle which can support society, and every duty of morality and religion?'

What a picture, my brother! could I suspect? – But I will continue –

'Good heaven!' said I, 'if such a man really exists, let him be an outcast from the society he has injured; let him first feel the effects of that depravity he has meant to introduce.' – 'Certain it is,' said Dr. C——, 'that some such monster the world has produced, and that this age, enlightened and refined as it is, has, in the work now in my hand, received and applauded the apology of a suicide, and, excuse me the expression, an adulterer also.' –

He opened the book he had taken from a seat near us: judge my surprize on finding it a volume of Werter, and that all this severity was levelled at that charming work and its calumniated author. It was not immediately that I could utter, and at length I will own indignantly, 'Is it then possible, my good sir, that even from the liberal-minded, that from you I have such an opinion as this to encounter? – an opinion, forgive me if I say' – 'And forgive me, also, madam,' said he, interrupting me, 'if I too exclaim, Is it possible that in a lady, and such a lady, so calculated to excite and suffer from all the passions raging in the heart of this Werter – that in beauty, delicacy, and tenderness, I behold his apologist?' – 'O could my expressions but equal what I wish,' said I – 'could I explain my ideas with that force of conviction with which they strike on my own mind, in me, sir, you would see that person – in me sir, whose frame shudders, whose heart revolts at the crimes you mention, you would behold that apologist.' – 'Did I not know,' said Dr. C——, smiling, 'that it is the province of the ladies to reconcile contradictions, I might be surprized; as it is, I am determined to be only attentive.' He bowed and sat silent.

My aunt, and the rest of the company in compliment to her, laid down their cards. How often had I wished for an opportunity of refuting these cruel and injurious opinions; but all the interest I took in the subject could not now raise my spirits. The attention I had unthinkingly centered in myself, covered me with confusion, which every moment of silence encreased. If all shame is false which arises not from guilt, I have very little excuse for that which at this minute so oppressingly distressed me.

My aunt took the only way of relieving me by resuming her cards; and Dr. C—— again renewed the discourse, by saying, 'You have heard my accusations of this work, madam; yet, so warmly as you espouse the cause of its author, I hope you will believe I am more desirous of having myself convinced, than of convincing you.' – 'I do believe it, sir,' said I: 'the candour which inclines you to that confession, must also incline you to wish such a writer as this before us freed from a charge so injurious to his fame, so derogatory to all that is most estimable in human nature, the desire of being serviceable to our fellow-creatures. In Werter we behold – Sir, you have read the book, I presume – some, I know, there are, who blame it upon reputation only.' –

'You do not address yourself to one of those,' said Dr. C——. 'Continue, I entreat you, madam.'

'Do we not behold in Werter, my dear sir, the ill effects which the gentlest passions, when unrestrained, may have on the best and most noble hearts? Do we not behold in him all that nature and genius can render deserving, wretched, forlorn, and ruined by one error, by one passion unconquered, by one wish imprudent only at first unsubdued? There may we not trace every step of the path which leads to guilt, to misery, to despair, and death? We behold the slow and almost imperceptible approaches which conduct him to the brink of the grave. We see him, my dear sir, all the powers of his imagination wasted – all the ties of religion subdued in his heart. Alone he stands in the world. The fountain of his tears, the source of his prayers, are no more. He meditates on murder and violence. He persuades himself that he is weak; he becomes so. He abandons himself; he is abandoned of the eternal.'

'How is it possible, my good sir, that there can be one reader, at whose breast this moral, this interesting moral, does not strike? How have I felt, how do I now feel it throbbing at mine! – Fly! it seems to say, ye children of innocence and peace, fly while ye are yet strong! O wait not till the arrow empoisoned, however distantly empoisoned with guilt, has spread its subtle and unconquerable venom through the heart! O wait not till that hour, which rapidly with the moments of time still approaches, when every thought shall be tinctured with some meditated crime – when guilt shall lose its horrors to your soul – and when, at length, abandoned by heaven and by virtue, by your own hand, in the blossom of your days, ye may fall – when ye shall rush through the silent and dark habitation, where the powers of repentance are lost – the curtain, which no more can be raised, is fallen for ever – unbidden, uncalled, in the presence of the Father of Righteousness, ye shall tremble, then polluted with murder, with suicide, at the footstool of judgment, at the tribunal of justice everlasting' –

The image which I had conceived was too terrible to behold: the cold hand of horror, which had thrilled at my heart, seemed to enwrap all my faculties: a dim faintness came over me, and before I found assistance was necessary, I had fallen. By the common applications I quickly recovered – the gentlemen had quitted the room, and Miss C——, supposing the heat had affected me, opening the windows, in a quarter of an hour I was well again. I saw, however, during the evening, that Dr. C——, avoided renewing the conversation; but when we came away, with the tenderness of a father he pressed my hand, and said, 'we must not talk any more of this for some days at least; besides, I know not if there be any occasion for it, as I question if you have not half convinced me already.' – He said so, yet many of the arguments on which I rest I have left unmentioned; but I hope to find an opportunity of conveying them.

Gently and tenderly as we returned home, my aunt chid me for suffering myself to be hurried away. I perceive, my dear brother, she has justice on her side; but in these moments to which she refers, I forget her friendly and necessary cautions: the object then present to my mind seems alone to occupy all its faculties, and it is not till the error overcomes me, that I perceive I have again fallen into it. Even now I have been in some degree committing it; and, what is worse, my aunt has discovered me; she has been in my chamber, and found me dedicating that time to my pen and to you, my brother, which she thinks necessary to my own repose. I promised to leave off, and therefore I cannot tell you what happened to us in our way to Dr. C——'s to-night, as I had intended; nor the attention my aunt seemed to pay me, when I just now reminded her of that end to my journey with which she once flattered me. Is it for me, my dear brother, whilst her tears of tenderness yet wet my cheek, to disobey her injunctions?

LETTER XXVII.

THE purple beams of the morning have this day displayed their beauties for me, as for thousands, in vain, and the hours which I have been accustomed to dedicate to instruction, have elapsed in insensibility and slumber. It is thus that fearfully and wonderfully we are formed. It is to this slumber, to this insensibility, if we would enjoy the one half of our existence, that nature obliges us nearly to dedicate the other.

Mr. S—— has sent an enquiry after our health, when it is his own in reality which was most in danger. I told you we were yesterday obliged to him for his assistance, and I will now explain to you how it happened.

In our way to Dr. C——'s our carriage, in one of the narrow streets here, got entangled with a cart, and through the ill behaviour of the driver was so jammed in, that we were apprehensive it would be broken to pieces, and ourselves crushed against the wall, or trampled upon by our own horses, who were not without difficulty kept under command. It was in vain that the footman, unable to pass to our assistance, alternately threatened and intreated – our terror encreased, and we heard the wheel of our carriage crash as the man again attempted to drive by us. I put down the back window to call for assistance. The people, who now began to gather round, at the sight of our situation, soon applied themselves to relieving it; and the carman, from his own whip, received the discipline he had with unnecessary and inhuman barbarity bestowed on his horses, who, seemingly more sensible than their master, had forborne to tear through all impediments. The cart was removed; but our situation, from the frail state of the wheel, which prevented the carriage from proceeding, was yet very disagreeable, the extreme dirtiness of the streets, the weather having been rainy, and the shower which was then falling, rendering it almost impossible for us to alight.

In this dilemma Mr. S—— very unexpectedly presented himself at the carriage side: his own, it seems, had been stopped by the crowd gathered by our disaster, and, understanding there were some ladies in distress, he came to offer his assistance. On recognizing us, he insisted on our making use of his. My aunt acquiesced, and having, by his advice, wrapped herself in a great coat of the coachman's, he conducted her first; when he returned, I was equipped in the same manner. But he expressed his perplexity at the risk I must run of being wetted in passing along the street, though a few paces only; and just as, encumbered with the coat, I was stepping out of the carriage, desiring me not to alarm myself, before I was aware he took me in his arms, and in a minute lifted me into his own: then bowing to us both, and pointing to his dress, which was by this time completely wetted, he was gone before we could make our acknowledgments; and it was in vain that my aunt entreated him not to run the chance of injuring his own health to avoid a little incommoding us; but kissing his hand, he hastened his pace, and was out of sight in a moment.

I have before mentioned to you the politeness of his address, and the soft elegance of his manners: I will own, that, to render him complete, he seems only to want some of that vivacity and fire which distinguishes that brother to whom I am too apt to compare all whom I have any opportunity of knowing. Are not our very ideas of perfection always swayed by the passions of the mind; or, rather, are they not formed after those images most dear to the affections of the heart?

I have been talking with my aunt this morning, and have repeated to her, a little more reasonably, as she called it, the conversation which passed yesterday between Dr. C—— and me. My aunt has one argument on this head which she thinks unanswerable; and that is, that the hero of the tale – Werter I mean – the moment he is most guilty, is made most to excite our compassion: his hand strikes the premeditated blow, and we behold him with more pity than abhorrence. But what other, my dear brother, what man less amiable, could so strongly engage our attention, or so forcibly point out that loss and destruction with which an object so excellent in its nature is overwhelmed?

She blames that idea of the rectitude of his actions, with which he is represented to be so forcibly impressed. I replied, and surely with justice, 'What, my dear aunt, would you blame that idea which strikes on the mind of the madman? Would you blame him, who, confined in a dungeon, and stretched on his pittance of straw, imagines himself possessed of the couch of magnificence, and the splendor of royalty? To me the situation of Werter seems similar; and, as I peruse those delusions of his disordered fancy, as I behold the pangs he undergoes, I look on him with terror and pity – my heart, in the language of Shakespear, exclaims,

"O what a noble mind is here o'erthrown!"[53]

I afterwards pressed my aunt to explain to me the reason of her avoiding those enquiries I have here wished to make. She answered me only by saying, 'I think, niece, there are few things I would not do to give you pleasure; and, perhaps, all may yet happen as you wish before our quitting this place.' – What is it that she means? and why does she yet keep me in suspense?

Here is another more serious circumstance which gives me pain – not a line, since I quitted her, have I received from my dear Ruth! Her silence gives me a thousand fears for her and her little Sophy. Sometimes I imagine, that, united to her Frank, she centers in him every wish of her soul, and every ray of her affection. Can she neglect, or does she disbelieve, that tenderness which I felt for, and which I so earnestly wished to manifest to her? Disbelieve it, surely, she cannot; and that she is capable of neglecting it, never will I believe it to be possible.

LETTER XXVIII.

HOW truly is it said, that by the loss, rather than by the presence, of our friends, we most discover the importance they are of to us!

We went this morning to the pump-room for the first time since Burell's absence, and for the first time also Mr. S—— was not there, who always used to join us a few minutes after our entering. The young men with great familiarity crowded round us, and one in particular disconcerted me by the impertinent and immoveable scrutiny I underwent from his eyes – from his eye, with more propriety I might say, since he, like many others whom I have seen, seems incapable of using more than one at a time, nor even that without the assistance of a glass. How despicable is that vanity, which makes even the affectation of infirmity a fashion!

The young soldier and his sister, whom I once before saw, were there again this morning, and, much I fear, want as well as sorrow sat on the faded cheek of the afflicted sister. I was prevented from speaking to them by the attentions and impertinent conversation of the coxcomb who had before disconcerted me. I must know more of their situation, and have now sent my servant to make enquiry after them. If, added to the ills of sickness, and the pangs of apprehension, they have any distresses which can be soothed by my hand, how joyfully will it be extended to their relief, and how willingly and happily employed in their assistance!

My thoughts followed their footsteps as they quitted the room, and I longed to be at liberty to enquire after them; but my aunt at that minute directed my attention to a person wrapped in a large coat, by the cape of which and the flapping of his hat he had concealed his face. He followed us at a distance during the whole of our stay. I remember that such a person Burell once observed; but, having fixed his eye on him, he mingled in the crowd, and we saw no more of him.

I could almost have persuaded myself there was something in the air of this man with which I was acquainted; but my aunt has ridiculed me so much for the supposition, that I have discarded it, and begin to fear lest he should rather prove some modest object of compassion. – My aunt, whose partial fondness leads her to centre all her ideas in me, suspects in him the spy of some lover of mine, or of the father of Mr. S——, whom she regards as such. I will own to you this supposition appears to me an unreasonable, and, from any other, I should almost call it unwarrantable, offspring of affection. Who and what am I, my dear brother, to be made of consequence to any but my friends by time and nature attached to me? And is there any thing in my actions which can authorise from any one the indignity of watching over them? –

This minute my servant is returned, and finds that this young soldier and his sister have lodgings at a small distance from the town, and that their circumstances are not supposed to be very easy. I must find some way of introducing myself to them, and I long till to-morrow shall arrive for that purpose. This evening Dr. C—— and his daughter spend with us. I will try, if, in the course of his practice, he should be acquainted with them: I might then better know how to offer that assistance and relief I may be capable of bestowing.

Miss C—— brings with her this celebrated Recess: she was reading it when I visited her, and told me it was a pretty thing in its way. If on reading I think no more of it, I shall have little idea of ranking its author with that of Evelina and Cecilia.[54]

I am going to employ myself very happily till their arrival, in completing a packet for you. My aunt would have me believe the pocket-book and ruffles I send you with it are master-pieces, and I can believe that they will not be indifferent to you, from the fingers which worked them. But you think I have no curiosity, my dear brother; or, after the picture I received from you with your last, surely you had not so long remained silent. May the original bestow on you that felicity which I so warmly wish you to enjoy! If she is capable of making you happy, is there any esteem, any love, which I cannot think her deserving of? Or, rather, is there any esteem which I can believe to be equal, or any affection which can exceed what her merit demands?

LETTER XXIX.

SHALL I ever be able to describe to you, my dear brother, all the ideas now floating in my brain, and the thousand emotions that are now throbbing at my heart – My heart! – How do I blush and tremble, when I would own to you, that at last it has felt – perhaps I ought not to express to you what it has felt – but you will be able to conceive its emotions, when I shall tell you, that, under the resemblance – the more beautiful resemblance shall I say? – of one by the ties of nature and choice first in my affection, I have discovered all the virtues most dear to my heart! How I have made this discovery I will relate to you; but I must first acquaint you I have read the Recess, and have been confined three days in consequence.

This morning, however – Shall I ever forget it? – Had I any suspicion, when I rose, of what this morning would produce? – Little could I imagine, that, in following the dictates of compassion only, I should find——But you will learn nothing from these exclamations; I will then try to be methodical.

I went out this morning for an airing. My aunt was not risen, and, as I am apt to be faint, I took her maid with me in the chariot. I told you, I think, I had found out the situation of the soldier and his sister: I was driven toward where they live; and as the house stands some little way from the road, I got out to walk to it. We were passing the garden hedge, when, breaking through the melody of the birds, the soft breathings of a flute exquisitely touched drew my attention. Ah! my brother, I was "all ear," and took in strains that "might create a soul under the ribs of death."[55] You know my partiality for that romantic instrument: it was from you, my dear brother, that I first heard all the enchanting inflexions of sound it is capable of.

I stood for some minutes, every reflection lost, every faculty but hearing suspended; when a girl, coming out of the house, desired to know if I wanted any body there. I don't know what answer I made, but I followed her in, and, beginning to recollect my intention in coming, was glad to be addressed by her mistress, a decent woman. I now enquired after those I had heard were her lodgers, and soon learnt from her the particulars of their situation.

Alas! stretched on the bed of sickness, to feel the afflictions of poverty, is there an idea of wretchedness beyond it? To weep over such distress is merely human; yet the earnestness of my enquiries, the tears that fell as she spoke, made her imagine I had some nearer interest in them than that of common humanity.

She was telling me, that, till within these few days, they had no prospect of relief, and was praising the hand which within that time had afforded it, when a scream from a further apartment pierced my ears. In a moment the young woman, whom I recollected as the sister of the soldier, rushed out with all the symptoms of despair in her countenance; and, wringing her hands, called for help, still exclaiming, 'He is dead! he is dead! he is dying!' The mistress and the maid of the house ran to her assistance, and I followed them. As I entered the apartment, I beheld the soldier extended and inanimate on the floor. After sprinkling some water on him, and applying some restoratives, which all but myself, overcome with terror, had appeared incapable of, I found he began to recover from what was only indeed a sudden faintness. His sister, trembling and almost incapable of motion, hung over him as she knelt at his side; her eyes, as in the agony of earnest attention she stretched forward to observe him, wildly fixed on his face, one hand eagerly grasping his, as yet unconscious, whilst the other pressed on her heart, which seemed almost bursting with terror and anxiety.

I can feel, but can I, my dear brother, describe her emotion?

When she beheld the first symptoms of returning sensation, she clasped her hands, she cast up her eyes to heaven, she would have spoken, but from her pale and agitated lips a few inarticulate sounds only found their way. I quitted her reviving brother, to give a glass of water to her: she drank it, and wet his forehead with the tears which now burst from her; and then again, as if unable to support herself, bent over him, like a flower that droops under the torrents of the north, and pressing his arm, 'You live, William,' said she, 'you live, and an angel from heaven has not come in vain to our assistance!'

I felt her situation too strongly, and now moved to quit the room; but she flung herself on her knees before me, and, uttering a thousand incoherent thanks, almost overpowered me. I raised her with difficulty: she kissed my hands, and, as I held hers, endeavouring to moderate her transports, looking in my face, and seeming first to recollect the strangeness of my being there, 'Ah! madam,' said she, with an expression of anxious curiosity, 'who then are you, and how – but I can guess – '

Her brother now faintly calling her, she broke off, and I quitted the room, and soon recovered myself. As I had been obliged to use some drops, I thought it better to stay, more thoroughly to recover and compose myself. I am seldom used to be so careful, but I wished to know more of her.

The mistress of the house, making many apologies for not being able to attend me, insisted on ushering me into her best parlour. On the table there, among a sheet or two of music and some writing implements carelessly scattered, I found the Tempest[56], and that beautiful and heart-rending poem of Falkner's, the Shipwreck.[57] I was taking up the last, when another book caught my eye – it was Werter. Under it lay a half-finished drawing. Werter was represented there by the side of his favourite spring, fixing his eyes, full of expression, on those of Charlotte. The stones, half covered with moss, formed the descent to the water, and the willows hung their dark leaves over the translucent surface. I had attempted something of this kind myself, but this a thousand times exceeded it;

and I felt a curiosity, almost insurmountable, to behold the person who had thus surpassed me.

Twice I rose to walk out in the little garden from whence I had heard the flute, and twice the consciousness I felt of wishing to meet this stranger detained me. – There are moments in which the heart seems to forebode the importance of the circumstances which approach; why else did mine at that minute flutter so ungovernably?

After having, for the first time, cast my eyes with indifference over some pages of Werter, I was laying it down with the intent of going out, when I was again stopped. It was not now merely by my own reflections; it was by the entrance of Joannah. You have yet known her only by the name of the soldier's sister. Again she poured out her thanks to me. I told her I should hope to be further acquainted with her, and expressed my regret at having so long delayed visiting her. 'The gentleman has been here but these two days, madam,' said she, 'so how should you think of visiting us before?' – 'Gentleman!' I repeated; 'what gentleman?' – 'To be sure, you know what gentleman, madam,' returned Joannah, 'or you could not, as I said, have thought of coming here.' – I assured her that I did not even know to whom she alluded. I told her my whole intention in coming there was to find her, and alleviate, if possible, her sufferings. – She now repeated, 'Not know him, madam!' with tokens of surprize: 'is it out of goodness to us, then, only that you come here?' – I repeated my assurances to her.

The modest effusions of her grateful heart at once pained and delighted me. I was incapable of stopping her, and she continued, 'O, madam! are there many so beautiful and so good? – My brother has been some months ill; he looks very bad now; but the Doctors assure me he is likely to recover – yet I was so foolish to-day, I could not bear to see him faint. – We have been in want indeed; my fingers earned us but a poor support: I was obliged to attend him too till this week, when the gentleman I told you of came – He is like an angel, more than any thing else; so good, so mild, so compassionate. The first night he was here, he saw my brother; we have wanted for nothing since; and I thought, madam, indeed I beg your pardon, but I thought you must have belonged to him.'

There was nothing in the idea, certainly, to be offended at, and I know not when I should have broken off the conversation, if the maid, whom I left in the carriage, had not come in search of me. She was alarmed at my stay, and feared lest my aunt might be so; but telling her I was well, and would soon be with her, I sent her back again to the carriage.

When again alone with Joannah, I took my leave of her, and, as she held my hand, I slipped my purse, which I had some time kept there, unknowing how to offer it, into hers, and, promising to visit her again soon, stepped as hastily as I could to a door which I saw open. I had got some paces from it, before I found it led a different way from that at which I had entered. I was looking if there was any path which I could follow, without returning through the house, when I saw Joannah's brother coming towards me; he was coming, but not alone. Shall I own the elegant, the more than elegant figure of the young man, on whose arm he leaned, arrested my footsteps?

Good heaven! will it ever be possible for me to forget my astonishment, when, as they approached, I almost thought I beheld the lineaments of your countenance, that expressive look, that air so peculiar to you, and so graceful?

I know not what I did – I stood still, I believe, gazing on the stranger; for I had not sufficient command of myself, at the moment, to avoid it. I saw him, my brother, whilst the glow of health and vivacity crimsoned his cheek, whilst the eagerness of surprize and curiosity sparkled through his intelligent eyes, attentive to the feeble and slow steps of the invalid, who was supported by his arm.

I cannot describe my perplexity, and scarce heard the thanks which the low voice of Joannah's brother attempted to express. I would have recollected myself; but the eyes of the young stranger, like a sun-beam, seemed at once to penetrate and dive into my heart – his eyes, my brother, I will own, I think even yours do not equal them – they are dark, and, alas, how piercing! – but there is yet something in them "so winning, soft, so amiably mild;"[58] in short, prepossessed as I was in his favour, and desirous as I had been of seeing him, it was not for me to resist them; and the almost wonderful resemblance which he bears to you, was scarcely necessary to make that impression on my heart which so strongly I then felt – the impression I am too conscious I even yet do, and perhaps for ever shall feel.

Why, as these sentiments arise in my mind, should I blush to commit them to paper? And what is there in this passion, pure and untainted as it glows in my heart, which is shameful to be acknowledged?

I was attempting to make some answer to the thanks of the young ensign, when his sister, the tears bathing her cheeks, hastily and eagerly joined us. 'O, my dear William! you know not half. O, sir!' said she, sobbing as she spoke, 'this lady is another of the best, of the tenderest' – 'Yes, madam! and this is the kind, the considerate gentleman – a few days since I had not believed there were two such in the world.'

'Two such!' interrupted her brother's companion, surveying with an intent look my embarrassed and blushing countenance; 'and is it possible that there are two such in the world!'

He understood, I am certain, the more than compliment which was intended to him; but should I own how much I was flattered by that which he conveyed to me; or was I wrong in acknowledging it by an inclination?

Something I said of having mistaken my way out, and, pressing the hand of Joannah, which would have borne mine to her lips, I desired her only to shew me the path toward the road. The young gentleman – I know not his name – overheard the enquiry, and, leaving Joannah with her brother, conducted me by the way I entered at.

As he walked by my side, I felt myself for a minute at a loss – it was not for conversation, but I wished for I know not what expression. I talked, and you will think not without emotion, of the scene I had just beheld, and that tender affection I had just been witness to. Some lines, from a beautiful manuscript poem I was once favoured with reading, recurring to my mind, I repeated them almost before I perceived I was doing other than expressing my own sentiments in the most easy and applicable terms. I often find myself doing this when interested, and I always am interested in the subject I am talking of, for on any others I remain silent.

As I spoke, I read in his eyes that he understood me: I continued – 'We should cultivate,' said I, 'the friendship of the unhappy; in doing so, we have the pleasing hope of relieving their hearts, and we are at least sure to soften and ennoble our own. We see, among the faculty, a thousand instances that a good heart, though more firm, becomes not less tender towards the sickness which it daily beholds, and which so many from benevolence and humanity only daily relieve.'

As I said this, we reached the road, and the carriage, which I had ordered to stand at some distance, drew up. With an appearance of surprise, he said, 'You walk no further then, madam.' – I said, 'I had, been absent too long already, I feared.' – He handed me in; but the maid asking if I had not my cloak in the carriage, I recollected the having left it behind me; and whilst the footman was dispatched for it, the young stranger, with one foot on the step, and his hat in one hand resting on his knee, continued the conversation.

Good heaven! as he looked up, how the clear brown of his open forehead, the arch of his dark brows, presented you, my dear brother, to my eyes! In the elegance of his figure, in the easy dignity of his air, I beheld your image. My cheeks glowed as I looked at him, and I do not wonder at his saying, 'That want of health should have called you to Bath, surely, is not possible; I will flatter myself you reside there.' – 'At least,' said I, 'I shall not yet, I believe, quit it.' – He was again speaking, when the man returned with my cloak. As he took it from him, I heard him say, 'Has the man flown for it?' When he gave it to me, – 'May I be assured you do not at least,' said he, 'leave Bath for some days only?' – I told him I had not any such expectation. – He retired from the door, the man put up the step and shut it, and we were gone in an instant. I looked out, however, to the spot I had left him on; I saw his eyes follow the carriage; he perceived that I looked toward him, and bowed; but we were too distant, I doubt, for him to see the waving of my hand, by which I acknowledged it.

I came home, and wished to think of nothing else: I wished, but in vain, to discover the reason of his residing in the retirement in which he is now concealed. I am not yet able to make up my mind, whether I shall – indeed whether I ought, dangerous as I find him, to visit Joannah again.

I lay my whole soul, in all its weakness, open before you. Why is it, that my aunt, by her raillery when I have explained the sensations of my bosom to her, has now taught me to fear her austerity, and to fly from her confidence? A thousand times, when in the warmth of my heart I have talked to her, with the cold and chilling aspect of indifference or serenity, has she listened to its emotions. She intended, perhaps, to subdue – alas! she has only taught me to conceal them. I know, indeed, that strictly speaking, it ought not to have this effect; but that it should, is only human nature, and 'tis in vain that we think to guide the passions, to subdue the errors of youth, without studying, and sometimes also yielding a little to its frailty. Such as we are, rectitude, in all its severity, is more apt to disgust than entice: we are overawed, we feel the harshness of its effect, and forget the excellence of its cause.

Whenever I think on this subject, I could shed tears; for I now feel from it, I have felt from it. When I was but yet a child, I had a favourite teacher; and, as nature put few grains of reserve in my disposition, I would run, in any trifling distress of my companions, any childish misdemeanours, to her – I would tell her our little distresses, and our little imprudencies, which a few falsities might have concealed. She would forget to commend that love of truth which really actuated me, and, attributing my confession to the fear only of being discovered, would reprove me with the same severity as if the faults had been denied as well as perpetrated; and punishment unmitigated was frequently the only effect I drew from my sincerity. – It is thus, my dear brother, that even now, when I express to my aunt all that I feel, and would paint to her all that imagination presents to me, she reproves or rallies me; and I have now learnt to spare her, as well as myself, the pain which I see my difference of sentiment gives her.

I have yet many things to say; but my aunt, who would never leave me alone, having had company, prevented me from sitting down to write to you till night: but I could not sleep without relating to you the ideas which now fill my imagination and my heart. I have related them, and the first streams of the dawn now penetrate my windows, and obscure the light on my table. – Adieu then, my dear brother. I think of you with a thousand emotions of tenderness, but to-night I will not promise to dream only of you.

LETTER XXX.

SLEEP and I have at all times but little to do with each other, and at present we have less than ever.

I rose this morning and went with my aunt to the pump-room. I saw and heard nothing there till the entrance of the young ensign and his sister: till that minute I had not known whether I wished to see them there or not. They came, and were as usual unaccompanied, and I then perceived too plainly the feeble satisfaction of beholding them was not all that I had hoped for. I conversed with them; but I could not ask, and they said not a word of the stranger – that benevolent stranger whom yesterday Joannah was so willing to talk of, and as such so desirous to introduce to me. – I was yet talking with them, when Lord S——, for the first time, addressed me. His son was not there, who has been indisposed, but he is recovering; and Lord S—— desired to introduce him to me as to-morrow. I thanked him for the honour which he seemed not to forget he was conferring on me; but remain as yet at a loss for the motives of it.

Lord S—— is one of the many who are very polite as far as respects themselves, but, as to those whom they address, much otherwise. He appears to imagine his superiority would be forgotten, if for a moment he himself laid the consciousness of it aside. – Alas! these children of vanity and weakness imagine they create respect where they excite disgust; and that mist, which conceals the error from themselves, increases its enormity to all others.

While I was ill, Lord S—— had before waited on my aunt; but I had made no enquiry about it, and now I only know that he interrupted my conversation with Joannah, who presently after quitted the room.

My aunt has just left me, and has proposed an airing, for which I well know her reason, as she will always find some method of drawing me from my writing; yet it is then that I most feel that bond of nature which draws me so irresistibly to you, my brother; it is then that I most feel, and that I most rejoice in that sympathy of soul between us, which enables me to acknowledge every emotion as it passes, every passion as it arises in mine.

We have been out, my dear brother: the choice of our route was left to me. Do you think I had philosophy enough to name any other than that of yesterday? Indeed I had not; and, shall I own it? I scarce wish to have. I thought the carriage would never come in sight of the house – to speak more sincerely, I thought it would never reach the spot where I last beheld the animated stranger. As we drew near I looked out. I was scarce conscious of doing it, or of the wish which I had formed again to behold him there. This wish, which, warmly as my fancy pursues every one which arises, amounted to suspence, to hope, to expectation. I was yet unconscious of its strength, till, casting my eyes toward the spot, I beheld its disappointment. We passed on, and lost sight of the house in a minute. We returned by another way, and today at least I shall live without beholding or knowing more of him who has thus intruded on my peace.

My aunt, who I believe observed my absence of mind, entered into a conversation with me, and talked of Werter and its author, and of completing all my wishes on that head. She then asked what I thought of the Recess.

I have not told you the story of my reading it. Two days ago, could I have believed I could put pen to paper after perusing that work, and have written so many sheets without expatiating on its beauties! – that elegant work, in which is united all that is most charming to the heart and the imagination! Its language, with all the fire and all the softness of poetry, conveys images the most enchanting to the fancy, and scenes the most interesting to the heart. Dr C——'s daughter brought it to me. I began it the next day, and, from the moment I first opened it, till the last sorrowful scene which closes that overwhelming narration of miseries, I quitted not the book. As I read, I felt all the pains of suspence at my heart, and I know not a term which can convey to you an idea how infinitely I felt myself interested through the whole: I was frequently affected even beyond the power of weeping, and scarcely could prevail on my aunt, with all my entreaties, to let me read the last volume: but persuading her that I should, perhaps, be less affected when alone, I had all the luxury of weeping over it by myself. I concluded it some hours before I attempted to rest, and then I started from my dreams, impressed with all the sensations I had felt so strongly in perusing it. Want of repose, and the extreme agitation of my spirits, produced a slight fever: my aunt thought it violent, and concluded me delirious; but a draught ordered by Dr. C—— soon composed me, and I waked from a sleep of some hours as well in health, and as sound in my intellects, as I usually am. Another day of quiet, however, was prescribed me: I obeyed, and till yesterday morning quitted not my room. It was then that I was permitted to make this visit I had before resolved on. When I projected it I thought only of the children of sickness and sorrow: I knew not, my brother, that the roof which concealed them, concealed also a son of genius and science, the pupil of sensibility and graces.

LETTER XXXI.

MY aunt cultivates a numerous acquaintance here. She took me this afternoon to Mrs. ——, a schoolfellow of hers: I remembered being once introduced to her at London. She is very gay, and there were several card-tables. Miss C—— was one of the company, and a Mr. Layton with her, whom I remembered having seen when I was at Dr. C——'s: I was put in a party with them and a troublesome coxcomb, who, since Burell has left us, contrives to conduct my aunt and me from the pump-room of a morning. He is one who joins great forwardness and affectation of manners to a most disagreeable and inelegant form, united to a countenance as bold as it is otherwise inexpressive. – What a contrast, my dear brother, to him whom I yesterday saw!

This strange being surprized me by enquiring of me after Mr. S——, who, he said, had been dangerously ill, he had heard, and that from serving me. Dr. C—— had told my aunt he was confined with a cold. I had felt myself interested for him, fearing it had originated from his politeness to us. I slightly, however, informed this coxcomb how far my knowledge reached on the subject.

He played with me, and we lost two rubbers[59], entirely, he told me, through my fault. Miss C—— took him in compassion, as she said; but it was in vain; Mr. Layton and myself beat them two others, and his ill luck, joined to Mr. Layton's raillery, seemed beyond his philosophy, and he gave signs of impatience and ill temper which a more trying occasion would scarcely have excused.

How many are the complaints of the crosses of life! And yet it is thus that out of nothing we create them, and multiply them upon ourselves.

Miss C—— is addressed by this Mr. Layton, and they are soon to be married. – I think, were I in the situation she acknowledges, I should not bear to see the man, on whom I was so near bestowing myself, sufficiently easy and disengaged to join in every laugh, or scarcely to rally any one. Happily Miss C—— is not of that opinion, and she seems fully contented with the homage Mr. Layton pays her, in allowing neither wit or beauty to any other woman. – I have met with some gentlemen, whose universal system of politeness to women seems to consist in this alone: their own hearts best know what are the passions which they thus mean to gratify, and what must be their opinion of the minds to which they thus address themselves. On what idea they would proceed I know not; but to me they are doubly disgusting, as I perceive their injustice to others, and, as I am certain of it in another situation, to myself.

We did not come home till it was late. I have not yet told you, that, in the course of the evening, Miss C—— asked me if I did not think the Recess a pretty thing enough. I was at some loss for an answer; but I conquered myself, however; and said only, 'Yes.' –

I once saw the charming author of this work, who was long injured in my opinion; I now wish to acknowledge my prejudice and injustice, and my present consciousness that it was such to her; but I am not to be so fortunate.

Miss C—— informs me, that she has set out on a visit to a neighbouring kingdom, where perhaps even now she wanders over the hills once marked with the footsteps of Ossian, and there, whilst the blast of the heath conveys his spirit to her soul, she contemplates those singular and touching graces of nature which she so well knows how to describe. For me, my dear brother,

> "Who feel, whene'er I touch my lyre,
> My spirits sunk beneath my proud desire,"[60]

when I began to awaken from the sweet delusion, that, guided by her, my imagination had yielded to – when I could behold it as the offspring only of fiction and fancy, I wet this first and most beautiful effort of modern romance with the involuntary tears of admiration, and thought of the words of Caracchi.[61] I will flatter myself, that something like what passed in his mind, when, on beholding the paintings of Raphael[62], the emphatic exclamation, "And I too am a painter!"[63] burst from his lips, at that enthusiastic moment enraptured my heart. –

How have I lost myself in my subject! I told you Miss C——'s question, and how I answered. I had reason to be angry with myself, when I saw Mr. Layton's face; and thought of what you once told me, when you said that my sentiments might be rather said to be conveyed by my eyes than my lips. He seemed hurt for Miss C——, but, happily for me, his confusion served to conceal that which he had raised in me. – He shuffled the cards that lay next him, mixed half of them with his own, and then, bursting into an assumed fit of laughter, said, he had lost deal. This produced a dispute between the two gentlemen, on which, what had really caused it was forgotten; and I felt myself obliged to Mr. Layton for the manner in which he had relieved me as well as himself. I was in fact to blame; for I should have known that in this age of science, of reading, and sensibility, numbers peruse what is publicly approved, only because it is so, and for that reason alone join in talking of writings and feelings, which they neither conceive nor understand. Miss C—— I imagine to be one of this class; but she was sincere, and expressed what she felt, and no more; and that ardor with which I would have spoken of this work, might have discomposed her as much as the coldness and the vagueness of her expressions did me.

LETTER XXXII.

I BROKE off abruptly last night, lost in a thousand conjectures when and by what means I should see more of that resemblance of you which has so much prepossessed me. The minutes passed unperceived away: and as I recalled the figure and the expression of every animated feature which had struck me, I wished to make out the reason of his residing where he now does; but only bewildered myself, and when I cast my eyes on my watch, an hour had elapsed.

It is thus that, on the wings of contemplation and fancy, the time of our being is borne away: alas! it is in the periods of sorrow we wish it to pass, but in vain: in the slow and lingering moments of anguish, we bewail the length of that span of existence which is allotted to us. I sighed as the reflection occurred to me. I kissed your dear little picture, and resolved to be detained no longer; but this resolve was made only to be broken. On my toilet lay some trinkets I had arranged there, and which I had purchased for my Ruth and her little Sophy. But why should I say *my* Ruth? I have deceived myself; I have felt a friendship which has not been returned; I have opened my heart to receive her, and she forgets me. I have written to her, but received no answer. My aunt triumphs over me, and talks to me of becoming wise by experience; but experience, my dear brother, it shall be. I will not trust to doubts after my second letter. I would have sent a messenger, but my aunt rallied me, and would not suffer it; but if this day passes and my suspence is not relieved, if she refuses that request, I will myself go to my Ruth – the world shall not detain me.

As I cast my eyes on the expression I have just used, warm as it is, I find, when I look into my heart, that it means nothing. I perceive too plainly, that the curiosity and anxiety I now feel only to know more of one inhabitant of a small and insignificant spot, is alone sufficient to detain me. I am determined, however, I will send to Ruth, and a thousand apprehensions for her, a thousand suppositions from her conduct, throbbed at my heart, and drove all sleep for some hours from my eye-lids.

I am not to go out this morning, in expectation of Lord S——. What have I to do with the formality of introducing his son? Is it not sufficient that my aunt should receive them?

I have breakfasted with my aunt, and my dress does not please her; it is too simple, I think is her objection. I am to set myself off, and I see my drawings laid about with an air of negligence. This I always hated, and now it is more displeasing to me than ever. I read something in the looks of my aunt which I cannot account for –

I was called suddenly away – I have been surprized, and overjoyed. A gentleman, was my aunt's message, waited for me.

How often has it been observed, how often will it be observed, that the mind, when strongly impressed with some leading idea, still connects every new one with that which already predominates there! It was so with me: my feet, "swift as imagination or the wings of love,"[64] conducted me to the room where I expected to see – Need I tell you whom I expected to see? – I opened the door – I looked, I will own, for my stranger, when, with steps almost as rapid as my own, Burell advanced. Disappointed, trembling, and agitated, I scarce knew how to receive him. The disorder of my countenance was in a moment communicated to his. I recollected myself: 'My friend Burell!' said I, as I gave him my hand. He recovered himself. My aunt expressed her sorrow at having so much surprized me; but the intelligence he came to communicate compensated, how much more than compensated, for it. Burell, I saw it with pain, gazed earnestly at me, and seemed willing to dive further into the cause of that involuntary emotion which had nearly overcome me. My aunt mentioned our expected visitors, and all I had before felt was painted in his countenance. He made some incoherent enquiries: I explained the whole to him. As he looked at me, his spirits seemed to return: he talked of my health, and seemed to sympathize in my pleasure, as he told me that these arms may again hope to receive, that these eyes may soon expect to behold, the restorer of my existence, my friend, the friend of nature and of choice, in you, my dear brother. – I perused the tender sentence where you mention your Theresa, and kissed the brotherly lines. I shall be all impatience till your arrival.

Burell did not stay long; he seemed disturbed, and I flew to my own apartment, where I look at your picture, and alternately write and contemplate it as it lies beside me.

END OF THE FIRST VOLUME.

THE

VICTIM OF FANCY.

VOL. II.

THE

VICTIM OF FANCY,

A NOVEL.

IN TWO VOLUMES.

BY A LADY,

Author of the CONQUESTS of the HEART.

_____

VOL. II.

_____

With frames and constitutions weaker than Men have, the passions of
Women are warmer; and the rays of their genius concentrate to the
object on which they engage themselves more strongly – it absorbs all
other considerations.

PROGRESS OF FASHION.

LONDON:

Sold by R. BALDWIN, Pater-noster row; and
G. and T. WILKIE, St. Paul's Church-yard.
MDCCLXXXVII.

THE

VICTIM OF FANCY.

LETTER XXXIII.

VINCENT BURELL, *Esq. to* FREDERICK BURELL, *Esq.*

"O! sweet to follow nature's powerful voice,
And make the friends of nature friends of choice."[1]

THESE were almost the last, soft, and energetic sounds which I caught from the most beautiful lips in the world; and but for them, with my few books, my drawing, and my flute, I could pass my time happily enough in the little retreat you have placed me in.

I had determined to be as reserved as you have been in trusting me with half your secret; but a day is passed without my seeing more of the angel to whom in my first lines I alluded, and I can debar myself from writing no longer: yet, believe me, I disapprove not in you what I know to be the effect of the most delicate honour and the tenderest affection to the whimsical lady to whom you have thought proper to devote yourself. For my part, I have passed fire through all the beauties of France, Spain, and Italy, from nineteen to three and twenty, without a flaw in my heart; yet here in a corner which, had I fled for security, I should have chosen, I must behold an assemblage of all that is enchanting and all that is winning in the soft graces of woman – I must behold the mild blush of modest benevolence, which shrinks from observation, like the first tints of the morning mantling on the cheek of beauty and sensibility. My heart was taken by surprize; and as I shut the door of her carriage, as I saw it depart, the last waving of her delicate hand fixed every link of the strong and irrevocable chain[2] which now binds me to her for ever.

When you read this, you will think it scarce possible for me to bear my confinement any longer; and I shall wish this Werter, of which I am to fancy myself the author, with all its beauties, in the bottom of the ocean, if it is yet to detain me here; and as to quitting Bath immediately after being introduced to your lady in my borrowed character, absolutely I cannot think of it. In short, I must know more of this charming woman; and as you leave me ignorant of your fair one's name, my remaining there may not perhaps inform me of any thing more than you wish me to be acquainted with. I will inform you how I saw this lady, and how I became thus penetrated. –

My lad, whom I had sent in for a drawing I had a mind to finish as I leaned over an old wall at the back of the garden, returned to me with a long story of the ensign, whom I think you know lodges here, having been taken suddenly ill; and that a young lady, who was come to see him, had been near fainting, and was now sitting in my apartment to recover herself: – he came back to ask me if I would have him go in. You know the curiosity one has, one knows not why, in a retired place to see people. I determined to go myself, especially as the maid said she was very handsome. I was just within doors, when the ensign[3] and his sister met me. We are already much attached to each other, and his sister asked me to walk a few minutes in the air with him, whilst she ran to thank the sweetest creature in the world who had come to their assistance. My curiosity was encreased; but Joannah left us, and I attended her brother. I am the confident of a passion of his, and hoped this might be the lady; but I was mistaken; with this lady he was unacquainted; he recollected only having once observed her on her being taken suddenly ill when he was at the pump-room. We just walked to the end of the little enclosure here, and he motioned, I believe out of compliment to me, to return. There is a small green between the garden and the house, which we were just entering, when, near the door, I saw the fair and elegant form which has enchanted me, simple and unadorned in a white morning dress, which left only her delicate hands visible. As she approached, her eyes were fixed on us; I had almost fancied they were fixed on me. We had scarcely reached her, when the sister of the young ensign joined us. In the overflowing of a grateful heart she broke in upon the thanks he was offering, and introduced me to the loveliest of human beings. I attempted to say something which might convey the idea I had conceived of her, and the fire which her fine eyes had lighted up in my soul. She seemed in haste to return; and the eagerness of my looks, I fear, disconcerted her. I accompanied her over the short meadow which divides us from the road; and could not refrain from fixing my eyes on her, whilst my whole soul was wrapt in attention. Her accents, soft, melodious, yet full of energy, are framed at once to awaken and subdue every passion of the heart.

When the carriage drew up, I felt chagrined and disappointed, and certainly handed her into it very awkwardly. Fortunately she had left her cloak in the house, and I gained a moment's reprieve, and stood looking under the white hat which before had half-shaded her lovely face from my observation – I will describe her to you such as she now appeared to me; I will leave you to judge whether she was to be resisted.

I will begin then with what first raised in me a more than ordinary attention: Her fine-formed shape, her delicate shoulders, have that elegant turn, that remarkable fall, which is so seldom met with, and which alone would give grace to a figure even less beautifully regular than hers: her complexion has that blue and delicate whiteness, which seems formed to discover, through the clear transparency of its surface, every emotion which passes in the soul: her eyes are bright, intelligent, piercing; I never saw any so highly animated, so lucidly charming: the beautiful arch of her dark-brown eye-brows rises through the blue veins which wander over her noble forehead, and add grace and expression to her whole countenance. There is, when she is silent, a languor in her fair face which wins, which softens, which attracts – which is, in short, irresistible – I have often thought of it, since she quitted me – and the sweet glow on her cheek was, I fear, rather the blush of sensibility than health – yet that clear and rosy redness of her mouth, her beautiful mouth, formed on the most enchanting model of love, surely it must be the tincture of health, as well as the criterion of loveliness – I will hope so at least – The profusion of her bright chestnut hair, in spite of art and fashion, retains that sweet waviness which shews the remains of its native beauties; while the silky brightness of those ringlets which are yet permitted to flow on her graceful shoulders, prove that to nature only they are indebted for their negligent and elegant curl. – While I beheld her, I silently applied to her the most charming line of the most charming poet in the world – a line which I can never remember without encreased admiration. The harmonious cadence of it suited admirably the flow of my ideas at the moment – Ah! – "A vermil-tinctur'd lip, Love-darting eyes, and tresses like the morn,"[4] indeed thought I. – I had not time to contemplate every beauty, but her whole figure, her expression of countenance, her animated air, is that in which a painter would embody genius and sensibility.

When the servant returned, I had just sense enough to ask if she resided at Bath. I bowed, and the carriage drove off. How I envied the beggar that asked a few halfpence of me, and then followed, without an idea, the vehicle which contained her! How I envied Villers and his sister, who the next day conversed with her! but she said not a word of me; and perhaps with this subject, which I could dwell on for ever, I have only tired you. I have, however, been very sincere. You find how it is with me, and you must know it impossible for me to remain here with patience.

I hope you are by this time at Bath, and returned from that attendance to your friend C——, which so unexpectedly and unseasonably called you away; if not, I have ordered the boy to come on with this to you. In retiring here I satisfied your over delicacy shall I say? – yet to that perhaps I owe the having seen the lovely woman who has subdued me; at least, I should not otherwise have seen her in that winning and amiable light in which she here presented herself to me.

Send me an answer directly, or come yourself, that I may consult with you on fulfilling your schemes, but, above all, on my own enlargement; yet believe me still at your command, and that I shall ever remain,

Your affectionate brother,

VINCENT BURELL.

LETTER XXXIV.

Miss MORVEN *to Colonel* MORVEN.

LORD S—— was here this morning, whom I think I mentioned I expected, and presented his son to me – presented him as a lover. Confused and surprized, I looked at my aunt: she was not ignorant that this step was intended, but in compliment to my delicacy she said it was that she spared me the embarrassment of knowing it. – Ah! my dear aunt, was it not that you rather suspected the refusal I should certainly have given, had you told me the intention of this introduction, as you called it?

I have reason to think I displeased my aunt; yet, surely, it was necessary I should be explicit in acknowledging how unexpected such a declaration was to me. Could I wish to appear to receive the visits of Lord S——, to make a parade of refusing his offers?

Something like this I said; but Lord S—— seemed to regard it as only the necessary language of a young lady on such occasions. I was going to reply to this insinuation, which I had heard but with impatience, when my aunt interrupted me, and expatiated in terms which confused me on the frankness of her niece: yet as she knew her, she said, to be wholly disengaged, there could be no impropriety in her having consented to, or my having received the visit – and concluded, looking at me, with adding, that having been till now ignorant of Mr. S——'s attachment, I could not possibly be sufficiently a judge of my own heart to give an immediate answer.

How I blushed, my dear brother, conscious of the weakness of that heart, and of the passion – must I say it? – already glowing there! I looked down, unable to reply, and in a moment my imagination was possessed by that nameless stranger, whose image is so strongly imprinted in my mind. My aunt kindly changed the conversation, and I beheld her ignorant of my real emotions, whilst a sense of guilt oppressed me at the reflection. – Apparently stupid, I remained lost in a variety of thoughts, till Lord S——, after a short stay, arose to take his leave. My aunt attended him out of the room; but his son, who had taken no more part in the conversation than myself, remained. He has been ill, occasioned, as Lord S—— had told me, by the cold he caught in assisting us in our way to Dr. C——'s. I soon recollected myself; but when I would have expressed the concern I really felt for his indisposition, he made light of it, and attributed it to other causes. – After some hesitation, he apologized for that abruptness which had been used towards me. The conversation became insensibly more interesting, and he at length made professions which pained me to hear, and more than once mentioned his hopes, from my being disengaged? He seemed to rely on that idea with certainty, and, as to himself, with expectation.

Surely, my dear brother, I was not wrong, though the sound half died away on my lips, as I would have uttered that perhaps he was misinformed, and, in short, I was not so free as had been represented to him, and as was believed by those who represented it. 'By acknowledging this,' said I, 'perhaps I may forfeit your esteem, but I shall be contented if I have reason to think I have preserved your peace.'

I will not pretend to paint to you his actions and expressions; they were those of astonishment, and, I saw it with pain, of disappointment. Overcome by surprize, he expressed himself only by extravagancies – whilst he lavished on me a thousand encomiums I yet blush at so little deserving. After some minutes, which passed in incoherent exclamations, he turned hastily to me, who, confused and scarce knowing what I had said, attended to him in silence. My eyes shunned his as he seemed to read the agitation which spoke through the varying crimson of my cheeks. At length – I will hope that you know me too well to attribute to vanity my repeating his words – after a moment's pause, during which he seemed struggling to conceal his feelings, he addressed me in a low but energetic voice.

'I am persuaded,' said he, 'that Miss Morven will forgive in me those transports I had too much weakness to conceal. I had flattered myself, madam; I am undeceived: but I yet behold in you, noble woman, all which my heart had taught me to believe you, the unblemished child of sincerity and nature, and ever inviolable shall be the confidence you have placed in me.'

I bowed and would have spoken, but with a quick voice he interrupted me. 'Miss Morven,' he said, 'your aunt favoured my expectation; let me appear to her, to my father, weak, capricious, all that is unworthy of you: what I am, let my actions express to you – your mind is too just not to believe them – your heart too tender not to pity me. – Sacred and beautiful drops! it is mine to excite you, it is another's to wipe them away.'

The tears had not overflowed my eyes, and I had flattered myself that he had not seen those weak and only tributes I could pay to his generosity. Again I would have spoken, and made him all the acknowledgments with which my heart seemed nigh bursting; but he had hurried out of the room. I stepped after him, however, to the door: he was standing too visibly affected just without it, and, when he saw me, was going; but, putting my hand on his arm, I detained him, and passionately I expressed to him my gratitude, my esteem, my admiration. – 'Lovely woman!' said he, 'and you forget that at this minute you are destroying me.' – I could say no more; he darted across the hall, and, flinging himself into his sedan, covered his eyes with his hand, whilst, filled with a thousand emotions, and happy to escape observation, I returned to my chamber.

During our conversation, my aunt had received a message from a lady of her acquaintance, who is ill here, and wished to see her. She is not returned; and, left to myself, I have sat down to transmit those actions and emotions, which so nearly concern me, to you. But I am not contented with myself. In refusing Burell I followed the dictates of reason and justice. I esteem him; I have even an affection for him; but never could I love him with that marked and decided preference which could authorize me to be his. Unbiassed and unprepossessed, such was my motive, and my only motive, for rejecting an affection which I have reason to believe so sincere. But it is otherwise with Mr. S——. I think sometimes, if I had not seen this stranger who has seduced my heart, there was something in his manners which might have won me. Not to reason, not to justice, is he then sacrificed, but to whom? To the acquaintance of an hour; of a minute I may say; and to the idle prepossessions of a fanciful and flighty being, misled perhaps by her own imagination – to the vain day dreams of a maid in love – a being unworthy of the attachment with which he has honoured her. – I repeat I am displeased with myself, my dear brother. I can write no more on this subject, and almost fear to think of it. I look at your picture and blush. I have acted, surely, in a manner unworthy of your sister – unworthy, let me say, of myself; and was my aunt here at this minute, I would lay my whole mind open to her – I would confess my error; and be guided by her directions. I would do any thing to be reconciled to my own heart.

LETTER XXXV.

ILL at ease, and discontented with my own conduct, I quitted my pen, and, seated at my music, I soon forgot every emotion of sorrow. You know my passion for the organ. There is a small one fixed in our apartments here, which was a principal inducement with your friend Burell to secure them for us. It is a fine-toned instrument, and when I draw from it the divine strains of Handel[5] – when, in a low voice, which seems to mingle with its sounds, I accompany it, my soul seems hovering on my lips; all that is earthly disappears from before me; the fervor of devotion rises in my heart; I forget the bands which unite me to mortality, and feel myself as if conversing with the blest of heaven! – To me, in the first harpsichord, there is some clash of string, which, like a bad actor in a play, reminds me of the mechanism of the piece – wrapped in attention, I have sometimes lost it in a degree, but never wholly – but from an organ every note is harmony. – As to a pianoforte, it may speak to the ear, but never did it reach the soul.

My aunt not returning, I continued playing, and was never in my life less inclined to disengage myself, never less inclined to think of that Werter, I have before so warmly admired, but Dr. C—— was announced. He complimented me in his fatherly manner on my execution. Perhaps, if in any thing I excel, it may be in this science of sensibility, and he obliged me to continue at my instrument. – I flatter myself that this worthy man has some partiality for your Theresa.

We afterwards fell into conversation, and, I do not know how it was, insensibly returned to the old topic Werter. He was almost as severe as ever to him: he talked of his cruelty and his crime to Charlotte, whose felicity he said Werter alone had destroyed; and had robbed her, not undeservedly, of the affection of a worthy husband, as well as the peace and innocence of her own heart.

But it was not Werter alone, my brother; it was her own want of prudence, of propriety, of strength of mind, which thus destroyed the peace both of Charlotte and her husband. It was no doubt intended, that Charlotte should be represented as culpable, and that in the highest degree. She it was who lost Werter to the world, to herself, and to heaven. She saw the passion which preyed on him, and repressed it not, till, at length, unable to be quenched, it destroyed the reason of her unfortunate lover. Flattered and moved by his affection, without intention of guilt, she suffered it to continue, till her whole heart was, like his, subdued. At the moment of first seeing him, she was, in the face of heaven, the wife of another: from that moment her crime commenced; and the fall of Werter, the distress of Albert[6], the failure of her own heart from virtue, were in that situation but natural consequences of giving way to the preference which she felt for him.

As I allowed one of them to be blameable, Dr. C—— was contented. Charlotte, he said, was, in general, thought innocent; but with me, my dear brother, she has never been accounted so: yet I own I admire in her that noble effort of the moment, in which virtue returned in all its force to her bosom, and triumphed there; and from that dangerous period she emerges like the sun from the morning mist, and rises superior to a whole life of cold and inanimate virtue, which, uninterrupted and unmolested, has kept the even tenor of its way. It is true, the virtue which has avoided, is more pure and unsullied than that which has resisted temptation; yet the effort of her who turns prudently back from a precipice, is by no means equal to that of the wanderer, whose feet, having slipped over a part of it, still descending with encreasing velocity, regains, by her own exertions, the right path in which she had at first trodden: – the former has avoided the danger, the latter has conquered it. And, alas! the frequency of those that fall, but too plainly evinces the imprudence of the trial, which to tempt is folly the most dangerous, and which not to fear is unpardonable presumption. –

There is nothing, I know, new in this simile; but I could not find a better, and Dr. C—— had the goodness to attend to me.

I thought at that minute of the numbers who fall and are lost in the devouring gulph of perdition. I looked towards heaven – children of error as we all are, my eyes filled with tears, when I thought of the severity which some of them experience. – I looked up towards him, who tells the sinner to turn from his wickedness and live, who strengthens the hearts of the weak. 'Be it mine, Father of Mercy!' said I, 'never to transgress thy laws; be it mine also to pity those who do!' – When we stretch forth the hand of compassion to the feeble, when we raise them from the gulph which should open to receive them, does it return to us sullied by their guilt, or does the tincture of their crimes overspread it? Let us fly their contagion; but, in doing so, let us not suffer it to extend to others; let us not, careful of our own security alone, suffer it to destroy for ever those who are already infected.

Once, my brother, I had the happiness to raise from the dust a daughter of imprudence and misfortune, and, removed from scenes where infamy was become familiar, her heart opened to repentance, tranquillity was restored to her bosom, and, with a small assistance, she now passes her life in that honest industry which once she conceived to be degrading to her. She has now learned the happy and necessary lesson, that, as no life passed in virtue can be contemptible, no one sullied with vice can be otherwise. At the time, my aunt, who is rather severe in her morality, blamed me; but a year has since elapsed, and I will hope not her expectations, but mine will be fulfilled.

I have run from my subject; yet that which Dr. C—— afterwards introduced was infinitely interesting, as well as distressing to me. He talked of the folly and the evil tendency of those books which set forth the violence of a passion at first sight, and the impossibility of ever subduing it. He treated their representations, generally speaking, as both improbable and unnatural.

On such a subject I dared not trust myself; I remained therefore silent, and he proceeded.

'They were passions,' he said, 'which were seldom known to exist, and, when they were, most frequently produced error and misfortune. They were, if ever,' he said, 'to be dreaded from those people who suffered themselves to be guided by fancy and imagination only.'

I was affected, as he pointed out to me the weakness I had felt myself subdued by – a weakness to which I saw his penetration made him fear I might be
sometime liable.

'Dr. C——,' said I, interrupting him, 'is a father: I revere his council as such.
I am the child of fancy, and my weakness is to be dreaded. I bow to the reproof
you now honour me with; it shall be my endeavour to profit by it.'

He seemed moved, and applauded that candor and openness to conviction,
which to forfeit is to become mean and ignoble; it is the weakness of ungenerous
souls. As he rose to leave me, he condescended to make an apology. – 'Forgive
me, amiable child,' said he, 'and do not say reproof, but advice: but where I see
the rare union of a person and mind so excelling as that of the lady's before
me, how can I avoid marking out that propensity which it is possible, and I am
assured only possible, might lead even with her to error.' – As he said this, he
kindly pressed my hand, and, unwilling further to distress me, quitted me rather
hastily.

Left to myself, tears relieved me. He knew not what then passed in my heart;
you only, my dear brother, know the whole of its weakness and its emotions,
which in all their folly lay open before you. As I recite them, I am displeased
with myself. The trial has come, and I have failed; but I am not likely to recover.
When I would contemplate your picture, another idea presents itself to me. That
dear and faithful resemblance, did I ever think I should behold it with regret,
with fear and impatience? But, ah! my brother, I feel it, mind and person; I am
not what I was. "Whence is this faintness in my feeble mind? Why has its noble
energy decreased?"[7] I know not why, but a cloud of melancholy hangs over me;
my spirits seem all retired to my heart; they are now only capable of increasing
its agitations; a languid fever at this minute presses on my faculties; tears dim my
eyes. I could almost persuade myself – but I shall hope soon to see you: I must
then be well; when I shall receive you, all sickness must subside, all emotions but
those of affection for you.

My aunt is returned; I must exert myself. In her presence I am always well,
but I suffer for it when alone.

LETTER XXXVI.

AFTER a succession of all the passions of the heart; alone, seated in the stillness
of the night, I watch over the dear woman who now lies sick beside me, and every
emotion returns to my mind.

Shall I not blush, when I recount to you, my dear brother, the deception,
which, trusting to my wild and ungoverned imagination, has been practised, and

has succeeded against me? I have discovered that stranger; to whom my soul seemed instantaneously, almost involuntarily allied, and I have found in him the brother of Burell. My eyes are no longer in darkness; I have beheld – but I will endeavour to look back with calmness, and describe the sensations which the past hours have given rise to.

As I cast my eyes on the bed at the side of which I sit, I feel them return with all their violence; I feel myself overcome by that torrent of tenderness and pity which breaks in upon me.

Forgive me: I perceive that I raise expectation in you which I delay to gratify; but with the slow and feeble expressions of my pen, I will endeavour to trace out the moments leading to that which now beholds me doubtfully and tremulously watching. – But I repeat I will relate to you all which has arisen in the past hours, the pangs which they have cost me.

When my aunt returned from her attendance on her sick friend, I left my pen to join her. She saw, I believe, the disorder of my spirits, and advised me, hastily I thought, to take the air in the chariot; and I, happy at once to avoid her company and observation, willingly obeyed her, and went out with my own maid only.

I speak sincerely when I assure you, that, perplexed with a thousand reflections, I thought not of the road I had been driven, till the carriage stopped, and Sally asked if I would alight. I felt my cheeks glow, and my mind irresolute, when I saw we were at the side of the road which led to the house where I had visited the ensign and his sister – where I had met – good heaven! how little could I have imagined it? – with the brother of Burell. I was sending in the maid to enquire after the health of Mr. Villers, when I saw his sister coming towards me. Her brother, she told me, grew rapidly better, and, mingled with a thousand expressions of gratitude, she told me, through the interposition of the gentleman, he had seen a lady to whom he had long been attached, and from whom he had carefully concealed both his passion and his sickness. He had hoped she might pity him; she had done something more, and, with the prospect of happiness before him, health seems to attend his wishes.

How I sympathized with the tender pleasure which glowed on her sisterly cheek, and sparkled through the drops of affection in her eyes! For once, however, I was prudent, and excused myself from stopping; but she would not leave me, till she had told me that the young gentleman was gone from them: she believed he would not return again. As she said so, I felt an involuntary pain at my heart. I repeated the words, and in a moment hurried away. Forgetting the little prudence of the moment before, I enquired if she knew where, but she could not inform me. A gentleman had been there in the morning whilst he was out with her brother; and had waited for him near half an hour with signs of the most violent emotion: he had then left a note, which perusing when he came home, he had immediately quitted them. His servant, she said, was to return and pack up what he had left behind, and she supposed therefore he was only at Bath. I had some command of myself; for I enquired no further. She quitted me, and the carriage was driving on, when a beggar, whom I had before seen there, attracted my attention. I stopped; I remembered him: he had once importuned me, and called my eyes from an object how infinitely more agreeable, how much more dangerous also! – But these thoughts, which occupied me on seeing him, vanished in a moment; I forgot even the cause of them, and surprize remained my only emotion. You shall hear.

As I held out my hand with a trifle to him, he put something into mine – it was a sealed paper, but had no direction. As I looked at it in suspence, he struck down a bye-path. – The chaise drove on – I opened it, and, judge my feelings, read these words –

"You seek the author of Werter: if you really wish to converse with him, to be satisfied of his opinions, his intentions, it is now only that you can be so.

To the world he will yet remain unknown; but seize the present moment, and to you he will stand revealed; at Bath you may now find him. Suffer your carriage to drive to the left side of the Circus[8], dismiss it, and a few paces will conduct you to the house where he chuses to remain unknown. The door shall be open; enquire for the stranger residing there, and your steps shall be conducted to the author of Werter." –

That project of enthusiasm and fancy which once so warmly animated me, had lain neglected; – but this billet in a moment recalled every idea I had cherished of discovering the author of Werter: It again seemed to occupy me with that force which in other days I have so often described to you.

I looked on the billet: that it could be a deception, never entered my head: I determined to follow its dictates. I did follow them, and beheld myself the dupe, not only of another's artifice, but of my own weakness.

I went, (forgive me, my brother,) I sent home the carriage, but I took Sally to accompany me. I had no fears; but alone to visit a stranger, something in my heart seemed to forbid it. I entered the house trembling with the eagerness of expectation, and made the enquiry. A female servant shewed me into a back room on the first floor. When she opened the door to admit me, I sent my eyes forward with a degree of earnestness which you may better conceive than I explain. I saw nobody; but she desired me to be seated, and left me, as she said, to inform the gentleman. I sate down in a chair which stood near a small writing-table, in a state of wavering expectation; – when casting my eyes on an open paper on the table, I saw it addressed to me. Is there a term which can express my wonder and confusion on beholding the lines which at that minute I perused, and here transcribe for you.

"To Miss Theresa Morven, – Forgive, beautiful woman, what an unconquerable and hopeless passion has inspired. Look not with eyes of aversion, but pity on him, who, *bound by no vows*⁹, wishes only to acknowledge himself as your admirer. Forgive, I repeat, the man who thus dares, yet dreads, to throw himself at your feet."

I looked over it in an instant, and, though I understood not the whole, I found myself deceived and entangled I knew not by whom. Trembling and indignant, it fell from my hand, and I hastily attempted to quit the room; but at the moment, rushing from an adjoining apartment, and impeding my flight with his knees, I beheld the figure and heard the voice of Mrs. Aylesby's Frank. I heard his voice, yet, whilst my astonishment and the confusion of my thoughts kept me silent, the words he uttered were lost to me. Some slight remembrances of my own, some suspicions of my aunt's which I had little regarded, now recurred to me. I wished to convey every idea of my soul in a look, and saying only, – 'Where, Mr. Hyde, is Ruth?' attempted to pass him; but he spread out his arms to detain me, and I was almost overpowered with the passions which swelled at my heart. I could not speak, but my silence expressed all that I felt. He let fall his extended arms, and, still kneeling, wrapt them round himself. My hand was already on the lock of the door, when his voice, in a deep and resolute tone, broke irresistibly upon me and detained me. His accents seem still to ring in my ears; and I shudder, as I repeat to you the dreadful words, which, like a bolt from heaven, seemed to transfix me. – 'Miss Morven,' said he, 'I seek not to detain you by promises you have a right to think false; I wish not to alarm you by expressions of frenzy, nor to shock your tender and delicate nature with the sight of me wounded and senseless at your feet; but fly me not, I conjure you, unheard. I wish not, I repeat, to terrify you; but the weapons of death are in my possession, and on you – on this minute only, depends the eternal salvation or perdition of the wretch before you.'

Terrified beyond the power of utterance, I turned – I beheld him fixed to one spot, the cold firmness of despair in his countenance, and no passion but horror seemed to remain in my heart. At once it seemed to swallow up every other before glowing there. A chill and overcoming damp spread over my whole frame, and dreading to retreat, unable to support myself, I sunk into a seat. – He remained silent, and seemed for a moment unconscious even that I staid, and I had time a little to recover myself; when at last, seeming to collect his faculties, he said, in a less dreadful tone, 'Miss Morven, you will then at least hear me.' Unable to contend with him, I bowed in silence, and remaining still in the same attitude he began to speak; but the intention he had hinted at recurred to me, and, almost incoherent with agitation, I asked for the weapons. He produced from his pocket a pistol: as he delivered it into my hand, my whole blood seemed to congeal. I laid it on the table near me, and, scarce able to support myself, leaning my head on one hand, with the other I secured it, as I paid that attention to him he had first insisted on my promising. After a few minutes profound silence, he addressed me: my agitation was somewhat subsided, and I think I can remember his words.

'You have condescended, or, rather, madam,' said he, 'I have obliged you to hear me; but in your countenance, so animated and expressive, I read all that I am to fear, and all I ought to have expected. Till the moment of executing the wild fallacy I have indulged myself in, I hoped I know not what, and till the instant of its completion I saw not all my error. Mad with a passion, which, from its birth, I looked on as desperate, I have forgotten the distance which every way must separate me from Miss Morven; yet, at least, believe me, that in pursuing it, madam, I have broken no vows' –

I looked at him, and my indignation now burst from my lips. 'You boast,' repeated I, with an energy which a moment before seemed to have forsaken me, 'that you have broken no vows, and you account then for nothing the abuse of confidence reposed in you by a sensible and tender heart! What is the breaking of vows – what are the ties of oaths, compared to that strong and indissoluble bond by which a feeling and delicate mind had united itself to yours? Your actions, Mr. Hyde, can only regard me as they concern my Ruth. Go then to her, acknowledge to her, if it be possible atone for them – '

He interrupted me. 'To her, to every one but you, madam, I can exculpate myself – to you, madam, only is my guilt; and by you, severe as I know your judgment, should death close the moment of my confession, by you, madam, I must be heard. On your promise have I relied; fulfil that promise; hear me only I intreat, and on your generosity I will endeavour not to intrude.'

Angry and agitated, I had risen, but again seated myself, as he appealed to my promise.

He remained once more for some minutes silent, only crossing the room in agitation; then returning to me he proceeded – 'Before I ever beheld Miss Morven, the tenderness which unsolicited was bestowed on me had awakened my gratitude, and till I saw her, the confession is already made, I believed it my love. – Hear only, I intreat you, madam' – (for again I was interrupting him) – 'your lips can pronounce nothing which your eyes have not already declared – Till I saw Miss Morven, conscious of all merits and all attractions but her own, till I saw her, with all the animation of genius, and all the softness of beauty, pardon me, madam, I believed myself Ruth's lover. Your aunt, in beholding your perfections, beheld also all which passed in my soul: I dreaded her eyes, and trembled at those of Ruth – yours how discerning, yet how blind! I contained myself till the arrival of Mr. Burell, but when in him I thought I beheld the favoured of your heart, I withdrew – In short, I acknowledge it, from that moment I have watched you, and have attended your footsteps. I have ardently desired, and have yet dreaded to speak to you. Undeceived concerning Mr. Burell, whom I had seen quit you, till within this week, I believed you wholly disengaged.' –

Judge, my dear brother, what I felt as he uttered these words. My heart, too conscious of its own weakness, caught the alarm; it seemed bounding to my lips – those lips which trembling refused their office, whilst my cheeks throbbed with the deep suffusion they underwent. But I soon recollected myself: I knew that what he had said could be surmise only; but the error which my soul acknowledges, my lips shall never learn to deny. I arose from my seat; yet, trembling with a thousand passions, was unable to move, but supported myself by the back of the chair, whilst he read in the struggles of my countenance all the emotions which I endured. He found I could not quit him, and again continued –

'Forgive, Miss Morven, the assiduity with which I have watched you, and the surmises I have dared to express. It was to-day, that, wrought up to madness by them, in the frenzy of a moment, whilst I trembled at declaring myself to you, I thought of the stratagem which has brought you to my presence; I have executed it, and am miserable.'

Can I describe my indignation, when I perceived, that, immediately on my departure from Ruth, he also had quitted her? I thought of the silence which she had kept; I imagined all which she must have suffered; and reproached my heart, which had accused her, perhaps, at the moment in which hers, too sensible and tender, was sinking beneath the disappointment it had experienced. I trembled for the delicate form which inclosed it, and my fancy already beheld her hovering over the grave. –

Trembling and indignant, I cast my eyes on Frank – I repeated her name – 'Ruth! dear and unhappy Ruth!' I exclaimed; 'it is I then who am to be your destroyer; and it is to me, thus glowing with the tenderest friendship of woman, that you shall be indebted for misery.'

I urged him to return, to fly to her. He was silent.

You know that energy which, surely, with the last spark of my existence, I shall preserve. I don't know how it is, but lately it seems to overcome me more than ever, and more easily to disorder my frame. I attribute to the varying sensations I had this day undergone, that I then felt myself ill.

The wildness of Frank's first emotions seemed to have subsided; tears fell fast on his cheeks: I again entreated him to think of Ruth, and, hastily moving from the place where I had stood, was leaving him. He seemed unwilling to make an effort to detain me, and I was on the point of quitting him, when the soft and innocent voice of little Sophy broke upon me. She ran into the room, and, flinging herself in his bosom as he knelt, exclaimed, in a voice of joy, that she had found her mamma's Frank, her dear cousin. I expected Ruth to follow her, and I was not disappointed. As she entered the room, my spirits seemed to return, and, reanimated at beholding her, hurried away as I am apt to be, I forgot the strangeness of my situation, and ran with expanded arms to receive her; but as I beheld her, she turned from me with a look of reproach, of disdain, almost of disgust.

At that moment, ah! my dear brother, there are no words which can express to you the pain which I experienced. I had flown to her with pleasure, almost with rapture: my heart was then throbbing with anxious and unbounded tenderness, and it was thus that she met, it was thus that she rewarded it. My spirits seemed at once to fail me; dizziness and confusion obscured my senses. She spoke not; but I answered to the thoughts she had too plainly expressed. 'Ruth,' said I, 'you are unhappy; but you are mistaken, dear Ruth, you have injured me.' – Her sensible soul read mine; she believed me; she pressed me in her arms, and the tears of noble and tender repentance wetted my bosom. Mine flowed with hers, and I was relieved. – 'It is not you, then,' said she, 'who have deceived me; I will believe that it is not you who have betrayed and have deserted me: but tell me, then, what am I to think? Is it Frank whom I must pronounce the murderer of my peace? Must I look on him as my destroyer?' –

As she spoke, I began to recollect myself; I cast my eyes toward Frank; I beheld him overwhelmed, almost insensible. He had not risen; on one knee he rested his face, which he had covered with his hands; but her voice, expressive of what passed in her agitated bosom, roused him as well as me – he lifted up his head. Shall I ever forget the object I then beheld? A cold damp stood on his brows, whilst on his cheeks and lips the last livid hues of death seemed fast spreading. He repeated the words which Ruth had uttered. His voice, low, deep, dread, despairing, it was the voice of resolute horror, the voice of wandering reason. An icy chillness ran through my veins; the terrified infant flung herself on her knees near her mother, and alarmed, she knew not why, fervently began her prayers. Irresolute, uncertain how to act, I stood gazing on each alternately. An instant had not passed thus when I saw his eye glance to the dangerous engine which yet lay on the table. The hint was enough. Swift as thought I darted across the room, and happily secured the pistol, and summoning all my resolution, with one hand, as he wildly seized the other, discharged it. The window being down, it made a violent crash; and the child ran screaming for assistance. Defeated of his intention, Frank flung himself on the floor, whilst Ruth, no longer able to sustain herself, sunk on the spot where I had left her. I returned to support her, and in an instant the people of the house came in. At their entrance Frank started from the floor, and was rushing precipitately from the room, when with a feeble arm I attempted to detain him; but he burst in a moment from me. Wild with apprehension, I addressed a gentleman I saw entering, and eagerly entreated him to detain this ungovernable man. He understood me in a moment, and, with address equal to his strength, flung himself in the door-way, and catching each of Frank's hands led him into an adjoining room, and, having turned the key on him, was at my side in an instant. But judge, if possible, my surprise, when looking in the face of him I was obliged to, I beheld that well-known resemblance of you, my dear brother. I started – I felt even then a lively sensation of pleasure at my heart; the sight of him for a moment suspended every other emotion. His astonishment seemed to equal my own, and an exclamation of surprize, almost in the same breath, burst from each of us. Burell, who now entered, seemed almost petrified with amazement, and I soon discovered the ties which bind them to each other. With equal anxiety they enquired into my situation; but, every possible emotion throbbing in my breast, I was incapable of giving them any explanation: I could only intreat their assistance for Ruth, and their attention to Frank. The first I had immediately conveyed to the bed, at the side of which I am now watching; Frank was left alone. He recovered from his stupor: all the atonement the past will allow of, he has made; he has sent the following lines to Mrs. Aylesby, by the hands of little Sophy: –

"If yet, injured woman, you can forgive me – hear, Miss Morven – receive my repentance, and I will yet live only for you."

When she had a little recovered, I read it to her, and she became more composed. The draught which was administered, has since taken effect; a long sleep seems to promise a restoration to her health.

What had passed in the presence of Sophy, had half broken her little heart. I had myself conduced to her sorrow, by neglecting to return her caresses, which, heaven knows, I was not conscious of receiving.

I have gathered from the child's artless story, the reason of Ruth's arrival at Bath, and of her joining Frank and myself at that period so unexpected. Sophy said, that her mamma had received many letters from me: she had often heard her say, Miss Morven would think her ungrateful, and would then weep, and tell Sophy she was too miserable to write to her, or any body; for her cousin Frank had deserted her, and was gone she knew not whither. She waited expecting his return; but, too much afflicted, at length she determined to come to Bath, where she knew I was, and to lay open her heart in my bosom. According to that resolution, she had come, and had just alighted from the stage, when passing the door of the house I was then in, my Sally saw her, and, knowing how rejoiced I should be to meet with Mrs. Aylesby, entreated her to step in. As they passed along the entry, Sophy caught Frank's voice: she informed her mother of it, and flew to meet him. – Can I then wonder at, or ought I to blame the suspicion, which for a moment sullied the mind of Ruth? – I who have doubted her friendship for that silence which anguish the most piercing has obliged her to keep. I now feel the injustice I have been guilty of, and bitterly do I reproach myself for it. –

My aunt has been with me here, and in as few words as possible I have told the whole to her, and her anger to Frank is great. She entreated me, however, at present, to think of my own health only, and endeavour at repose, and would even have persuaded me to quit the chamber of Ruth; but after all that has passed, fatigued and exhausted as I am, I feel myself too nearly the author of the misfortune of this amiable woman to obey even her: yet I have thought, as she bid me, of my own health; I stretched myself on a couch near Ruth, but was too much agitated to hope for a moment's repose. I rose and have written to you, my brother, till I find my weak and trembling fingers unable any longer to conduct my pen, and the dimness of my eyes increased by the intruding beams of the morning.

LETTER XXXVII.

WHEN I closed my last letter, the excessive weariness which pervaded my whole frame, seemed the forerunner of some approaching and violent sickness; but four and twenty hours since past in tranquillity and rest, have reinstated me. – The gentle and unremitting slumber which Ruth had enjoyed during the night, relieved my heart from much of its anxiety, and, when incapable of remaining longer near her, I reluctantly confided her to other attendance: a long and placid sleep succeeded those tumultuous hours which had disordered me; and I can now explain to you what brought the younger Burell and his brother to my assistance.

Good heaven! when so unexpectedly I beheld the former, and understood the union between him and your friend, a foreboding pang, why should I deny it? wrung this weak and too susceptible heart. I felt, in a moment, all the force of my capricious preference, and all its ingratitude – I felt it even then, when all the terrors of the tenderest friendship were beating with destructive violence through every pulse of my frame.

Burell and his brother, as my aunt tells me, had been with her almost from the moment, when, following her advice, I got into the chariot which had just brought her home. She had said nothing to me of Burell's brother, or his intended introduction, and now speaks of him as just arrived at Bath. –

I am always deceiving myself; but surely she saw my embarrassment, and even seemed, I could have fancied, to partake in it.

What means this air of mystery which surrounds this too attractive young man? – But I will proceed.

By whatever chance it happened, they were, however, with my aunt, when the carriage returned without me. The unusualness of my sending it home, I might have known, had I a moment reflected, would awaken in my aunt that tender and anxious curiosity which proved in reality the consequence of it. The evening drew on: the time, which with me insensibly elapsed, with them passed with all the tediousness of apprehension. I had given no message where to be found, and I returned not: Burell, partaking in her anxiety, and willing to relieve it, with his brother, came in search of me: they arrived at the place where the servants told them I had been set down, at the moment that the report of the pistol which I fired had gathered a crowd round the house I was in. It attracted their attention also; and the voice of my Sally, who had ran screaming for assistance, reached Burell. There needed no further inducement to him; but making his way through the crowd, he soon found the scene of confusion which plunged himself as well as his brother into astonishment. For my own part, affected almost equally by my fears for Ruth, and the emotions of my own heart at their unexpected appearance, by what I gather from my aunt, I must have spoken and acted with strange incoherency. Burell, however, procured the necessary accommodations for Ruth in the house, and that flattering repose which she has since enjoyed, has been succeeded by all the restoration of spirits which can in the present state of her mind and affections be expected.

I was not deceived when I thought her possessed of a feeling and noble soul: I repeat it, she looks on me with that generous partiality which is the offspring only of sensibility and gratitude, and her gentle heart rather regrets than resents the unworthy conduct of her Frank. When I would have expostulated with her for not confiding to me that suspence which has visibly preyed on her, It seems to me, said Ruth, casting up her eyes, which beam with all the softness of her soul – it seems to me, Miss Morven, but a selfish motive by which we are actuated, when we impart our sorrows to those friends who can sympathize in them. We relieve ourselves, but we forget that we are oppressing another. No, let me participate all my pleasures with my friend, but the moments which I pass in misery, them let me learn to bury in my own heart. My silence might injure me in your opinion; but I trusted that the moment would yet come, when you should be undeceived.

Amiable Ruth! I pressed her to my bosom, whilst my heart applauded, and for ever appropriated the sentiment she had uttered. She has yet acknowledged, that, when she unexpectedly found me in an obscure lodging-house, with that air of secrecy which surrounded me, she believed me capable, and thought she beheld me guilty of deceit; but the next moment, with an ingenuous belief worthy of a mind conscious of its own sincerity, she did justice to my feelings and her own: she has even acknowledged, that, at the time she set out for Bath, something like a doubt had arisen in her mind, and urged her to the journey; but in that doubt Frank only was involved; and with that modesty which characterizes and renders her dear to me, she added, 'I blamed him *then*, even for nothing so much as his cruelty in not writing – I thought it probable and natural, that to continue to love me, he should never have seen Miss Morven.'

Such, my brother, is the heart which he has wounded, and such the merits he could slight. – How often are women branded with affectation and insincerity for rejecting the affection to which their hearts are sensible, and assuming a coldness when they scorn to feel it; yet, when they give way to their native candour, it is thus they must expect to be rewarded.

> "That heart is ever lightly priz'd,
>   Which is too lightly won;
> And long shall rue the easy maid,
>   Who yields her love too soon."[10]

Whether the reasons from which this rule arises are right or wrong, I leave it for others to determine: for my own part, I believe they are, and perhaps ought to be, without an exception.

Frank has again written; he has not yet seen this injured woman: he urges an interview, and talks of absenting himself for a twelvemonth, when he may return more worthy of her, and less covered with confusion; at present, he says, with some delicacy, he deserves not to be united to her. I acknowledge I think it a happy and necessary expedient: he is less capable of propriety than I even yet believe him, if he avoids not all recapitulation. I believe I have mentioned to you my aunt's resentment. I could scarcely pacify her, and it was at length with much difficulty that I prevented her from seeing Frank, and expressing the reproaches, which however deserving of, he is at present unfit to hear. Her anger is increased by finding the affair has made a noise in the town. It will occasion, in all likelihood, our quitting Bath. Could I, my brother, quit with it every emotion I have here first experienced, how ardently would I join my wishes to be absented from it for ever!

_____

LETTER XXXVIII.

THIS evening Ruth has accompanied me to my aunt's. Frank has seen and taken leave of her. I was not present, but she has related what passed to me with the frankness which first enchanted me. He has erred, but his soul is not ungenerous. Penetrated, overcome by the condescension with which she listened to him, he wept on the hand she extended to him, and pronounced on it a vow, the most tender and solemn, to render himself by the future worthy of the confidence she was yet willing to repose in him. He talked of shortening the time of his absence some months, and is now travelling to the north of England, where he has some affairs to settle. He is to correspond with Ruth, and leaves to her the time of his return.

It was in vain, as she repeated to me every little circumstance so interesting to her affections, that she endeavoured to conceal her tears, till the sympathizing drops which they produced in the eyes of her little darling made her conquer them. At that moment, how strongly a reflection occurred to me, which I have before a thousand times made, yet never can I cease to wonder at the occasions which give rise to it: I mean that wonderful inattention to children, with which the generality of people are infected. How many parents, how many mothers, even, they who behold the first approaches, how infinitely rapid, of infant reason, yet remain insensible of that curious attention to every transaction before them which children and almost infants do undoubtedly pay! They see not how soon the feelings are awakened, and that talent of observation implanted in us by heaven is called forth. Even this amiable Ruth, whose life has almost been devoted to her child, hears with surprize those remarks which her emotion and the absence of Frank give rise to. For my part, I am convinced, that, were this power of comprehension, this susceptibility of impression, which pervade them, with regard to every thing more frequently attended to, we should find the years of childhood much abridged, and the character formed at an earlier period than we too generally behold it.

You may wonder, perhaps, at this observation from me, so little as you may think me versed in the œconomy of children; but much of it I had an opportunity of learning, even when excluded from the world, by the method pursued in the education of those children received into the house I was in: and once I knew a secret of importance divulged by its having been related in the presence of a child, who it was supposed would have been incapable of comprehending, and consequently of relating it. This idea has obtruded itself almost irresistibly on my mind; and, perhaps, whilst I communicated it to you, it relieved me a moment from others more interesting and more painful.

LETTER XXXIX.

THESE conflicts, my dear brother, I am not formed to endure: I am even convinced, if frequently I experienced them, they would abridge the hours, perhaps the years of my existence. In saying that my heart owns, that it seems oppressed by the generosity of your Burell, I feel how inadequate is all expression, how cold and inanimate to the sentiments with which he has inspired me – but I will explain myself.

Till this morning I had not seen Burell since our meeting so unexpectedly. My aunt had informed me of his anxiety and tender enquiries; I had even heard the voice, I had marked the footsteps of his brother, under her roof; that voice – why is the sound of it so pleasing to my ear? – Why are the feelings it gives rise to so prevalent in my heart? But, for the present hour, my thoughts ought to be, they shall be sacred to my friend. I will return then to the subject on which I first began.

This morning I quitted my chamber – Ruth yet remains confined to hers – and breakfasting with my aunt in the small room she has appropriated for that purpose, she shewed me a note she yesterday received from Lord S——. It informs her, with many apologies, of his son's having precipitately quitted Bath, and of his intention of following him, by which he was prevented from waiting on my aunt. He accuses his son of caprice and unpoliteness; my aunt joined with him, and, as things appear, not without justice. You know me incapable of affecting a surprize I could not feel. My aunt's chagrin seemed increased by my refusing to join in her anger against this young man.

Ah, noble S——! I feel all the merit of your sacrifice, and hardly can I conceal it from others. Surely I was born to receive and be sensible of the highest obligations, yet to sink under the incapacity of repaying them!

Involuntarily my heart made the apostrophe. I know not to what motive my aunt attributed the sensations which I could not wholly conceal. I had risen early; my aunt generally does; yet breakfast was scarcely removed, when I heard the voice of Burell, and in a minute after he entered. Little did I think on the errand which had that morning awakened him. Could I yesterday have seen a few hours beyond that in which Frank took leave of Mrs. Aylesby, what a night had I passed!

Unhappy Frank! I have not told you, that, before his departure, he sought my aunt, and left in her hands a few lines to me; they are such as became him to write, and such as did not pain me to receive.

My aunt was as much surprized as myself at this early visit of Burell's: for my part, I knew not what to think of it. I looked when other steps should follow his: the idea filled my mind, and rendered me confused, agitated, and inconsistent. With a look of deep concern, Burell enquired after my health; a look which seemed to say he beheld and felt for its decline. I recovered myself, and received him with that friendship which my heart experiences; which, whilst any of its powers shall remain, it must experience for him.

Breakfast was recalled; he spoke little; but there was too much expression in his eyes for the peace of your Theresa. I endeavoured for spirits which once were said never to fail me, whilst with difficulty those tears were restrained which the concern written in his countenance gave rise to. With an absent air he drank one dish of tea only, and then rose and crossed the room two or three times without speaking, took up a book which lay on the table, opened it, turned over several pages, and then flung it down. My aunt, as well as myself, saw in him an agitation for which she was incapable of accounting. We both looked earnestly at him; and Burell, recollecting himself, in a low voice addressed her – 'I have many pardons, madam, to ask of you,' said he, 'for the strangeness of my behaviour;

forgive me that I have no better command of myself. Shall I trespass too much on your goodness, and on that of Miss Morven, when I entreat, as a friend only, half an hour's conversation with her alone?' – 'The granting of your request,' said my aunt, 'lies only with Theresa. I can only say, that, when again you ask any thing relating to her, till you can better conceal the confusion of your thoughts, you must be contented if there is but one person in the world deceived by your requiring it as a friend only.' – 'Alas! madam,' said Burell, as he conducted my aunt, who had risen to quit us, to the door of the apartment, 'would to heaven that I could deceive even myself!'

Surprized at Burell's request, uncertain as to its intent, and doubting whether I ought to grant it, I had risen. As he returned, I would have spoken, but he interrupted me. – 'Theresa,' said he, 'it was in this room – I behold it with pleasure – you first allowed me to call you by the name of friend; I would speak to you as such. My heart is full even to agony: suffer me, at least, to pour out its sorrows in your bosom, Theresa. It is pressed with doubt: when the suspence is past, I know I shall better command myself; at least I shall be incapable of distressing you.'

He led me to a seat, and took his own near me, and we remained silent, till, hoping a little to relieve his inquietude, I addressed him. – 'I know,' said I, 'how incapable you are of wishing to distress me; yet, my friend, you do distress me, and, even at this minute, the words which you cannot utter without faltering, seem to pierce me, and, believe me, they have wounded my heart. For my peace, Burell, abate a little of that tenderness for me, which in destroying your happiness, must necessarily diminish mine.'

He once more rose, crossed the room, and, for some minutes, resting his forehead and eyes on his arm, which he leant against the sash, seemed incapable of speaking. 'At length, Miss Morven, I am weaker than I believed myself,' said he, as he approached me: 'it was in this room, suffer me to repeat it, that you permitted me the title of your friend; and this is the spot where so generously you promised me your confidence also on the most important event of your life. You will forgive all the emotion of your friend, when I tell you that it is to claim the performance of that promise I have now intruded on you.'

Ah! my dear brother, that flash of electrical fire, which, falling from heaven, in a moment can put a period to existence, pervades not with more rapidity and violence the frame which it destroys, than this explanation of Burell's, equally sudden and unexpected, did mine. I saw the cruelty of an answer from me, and dreaded to be candid; yet my heart, which revolts at dissimulation, seemed to hover on my lips. Again I thought of my injustice and caprice, and, incapable of utterance, I would have risen; but the attempt served only the more to discover my confusion, and trembling I resumed my seat. I felt the force of my own silence, and endeavoured at articulation. I looked up at Burell, who, with his arms folded, stood earnestly marking my countenance; and there, in the tumults

I endured, read the certainty of my affections belonging to another. Alas! when I beheld his, how bitterly did I reproach myself! The tears of a manly and sensible soul, how infinitely affecting! I saw the large drops trickle down his cheeks; I saw him scarce able to support himself, and my powers returned. I started up, and stretched out my hand to him: he flung himself on a seat, and his pale cheek rested on my shoulder: he took the hand, which hung almost lifeless beside me, in both his – 'Be not concerned for me, Theresa; it is past: but we must expect a pang at the departure of the last ray of hope, as well as the last pulse of existence. – Theresa, you pity me; but be comforted; my brother doats on you to distraction, and, believe me, he is deserving of you. I will quit you both, and you shall be happy.' –

Surprize for a moment overcame me; but viewing him with admiration, at length, 'Burell,' said I, catching his hand, and pressing it to my heart, 'it is impossible; I should then follow the impulse of passion only, and your esteem for me must be forfeited. Undeserving as I have proved myself of that exalted affection you bestow on me, trust to my regard, my admiration; it will in time make me worthy of you. Trust to that, Burell; accept of my hand in the presence of heaven, of my vows at his everlasting altar, and I will be yours.'

He rose with impetuosity, and caught me sinking in his arms. My heart, which a moment before seemed bursting, was relieved by tears; and I poured them without a blush on his generous bosom. I began a little to recover myself, and he remained still silent; but I felt myself infinitely disordered – my mind seemed in I know not what confusion – I would have given the world to retire, but I was incapable of even uttering the wish which I formed to do so. Tears again relieved me: I sunk into a chair, and Burell threw himself at my feet. He took both my cold and trembling hands in his. 'Compose yourself, lovely woman! Think not of me, Theresa: the struggle is past. Think of that delicate frame which this energy destroys. There are no words which can express my feelings at this moment; but your angelic soul is formed to conceive them: you can feel the motives on which I can refuse this noble sacrifice. Yes, Theresa, I do refuse it. The struggle, I repeat, is over; the moment of danger is past. If at first I yielded to the transport which it inspired, I will flatter myself it was not for human weakness to resist. But you will not now reject my vows, vows of everlasting attachment, of friendship, which life only can dissolve, and which no other woman can ever participate' –

He spoke with an agitation which increased my distress: he saw it, and quitting my hands, rose and left me with precipitation. I felt myself relieved, and indulged with more freedom my tears. In a short time, however, he returned, and my aunt with him. I drank a glass of water and some drops, and my spirits revived; but the sight of Burell pained me. I rose to retire. 'Forgive me, Miss Morven,' said he, 'if in the presence of your aunt I detain you a few minutes longer.' Hurried away by other passions, I have as yet not even mentioned what brought me here thus early and unceremoniously. Much as my curiosity was excited, there seemed, at that moment, nothing in the world sufficiently interesting to engage my stay. Almost unable to make an apology, I was going, when I thought of you, my dear brother, of your expected arrival, and resumed my seat.

'For what I have to say,' said Burell, turning to my aunt, 'I have your excuse, madam, or at least Miss Morven's, to ask. You must forgive me, if, as a friend, I have interested myself in her injuries; I have thought it incumbent on me to revenge them – '

'What is it you mean?' interrupted my aunt. 'Surely you have not followed and thought of revenging yourself on Frank!'

Too much affected before, what Burell had said had made little impression on me, till my aunt's exclamation roused me. Those murderers, who are suffered to exist undishonoured in society, under the name of duellists, have ever inspired me with horror. I looked at him, whilst that chilling sensation took possession of my heart, and spread itself over my languid countenance. He saw it, and hastily said, 'Do not terrify yourself: my hands, Theresa, are not defiled with blood: the existence of Frank is not in danger; he is safe, and you behold me also unhurt.'

My heart was lightened of the load with which his former words had oppressed it. 'Ever,' said I eagerly, 'ever, Burell, may they be free from it! Tremble, my dear friend, with me at that just, that dreadful sentence which pronounces, "Whoso sheddeth the blood of man, by man shall his blood be shed."[11] Forget not the terrors with which it will one day present itself to the minds of the guilty. For me it is that you have incurred this: alas! Burell, what more is it on your account that I must have to reproach myself?'

My aunt blamed my earnestness, and I had scarce finished speaking, before I felt myself its impropriety, and perhaps its cruelty to Burell. 'You feel every thing so forcibly,' said my aunt, 'you do not see how you thus distress all to whom you are most dear. You know her method of expression, Mr. Burell, too well to think much of it. I intreat you, for heaven's sake, to satisfy my impatience.'

'You had never,' said Burell, 'heard this from me, but for an accident which has rendered it public, and which made me fear lest it might reach you with exaggerations by some other channel. I have erred with the rest of the world, and, from the moment the whole of Mr. Hyde's behaviour was known to me, I determined to call him to some future account in the way which that world sees without abhorrence. I was misinformed of the time of his departure, or the hour in which he took leave of Mrs. Aylesby had been the last of his safety. I heard not of it till late yesterday evening. I then followed, traced him, and put up at the same inn. I did not go to rest, but waited with impatience till day should appear, which it no sooner did, than I knocked at his chamber door, for which I had purposely enquired. He was risen, and, on opening it, saw me not without astonishment. A few minutes was sufficient for my explanation. I was not very cool, but requested him to follow me. He seemed to hesitate a little, but at last turned resolutely to me, and said, 'I think, Mr. Burell, you are the friend of Miss Morven's brother; you, perhaps, I may therefore allow to have some right to the satisfaction you think proper to demand; but I was never more surprized, and never less prepared, that this morning for such a call.' I heard this speech not without contempt. We loaded our pistols, and sallied out. It was the first, and, I think, Miss Morven, it shall be the last attempt of my life of this kind. We went to a bowling-green behind the house. He insisted on my firing first. The ball of my pistol tore a piece from his coat, but he was not hurt. I then stood to receive his fire, but he flung his pistol on the ground and came up to me – Good God! I yet feel my astonishment, as I recollect his action and his expressions – 'I have no malice to you, Mr. Burell,' he said: 'your resentment is just, and you see no coward at your side. I have fought in this cause before, and, I am sorry to say it, yesterday evening, on this very spot, I wounded my man – '

Both my aunt and I interrupted Burell with repeating his words – 'fought in this cause before, and had wounded his man!' – I thought I should have sunk from my chair. My aunt gave me another large glass of water, and entreated Burell to proceed –

'Ah! Miss Morven,' said he, 'I should first have confided to your aunt; I should have left to her the unfolding it to you: upon me it is a task how very severe! But be not alarmed, I intreat you; be assured there is no life in danger.'

Burell then continued: 'I was struck' said he, 'with this address, and the information which it conveyed. It was in vain that I urged him to take his stand against me; he insisted only on my going in with him, and said he would then explain the whole to me. The affair could not have been long over when I had arrived at the inn, but I had shut myself from all society.' –

Burell now again stopped, visibly struggling for composure. My aunt intreated him to proceed.

'Be assured, I conjure you,' he continued, 'that no one is materially injured.'

Oh! my brother, I saw it was me for whom he feared, and for whom only he felt; yet I then knew not all my obligations to him: but I will continue in his words.

'I followed Frank in; he shut the door of his apartment as we entered, and then related to me all that had before happened. He had yesterday evening travelled but a few miles, when a gentleman rode up, accosted and accompanied him to this house. No sooner had they alighted, than he insisted on seeing him (Frank) alone. It was then the impetuous young man informed him of the intention with which he had joined him, and, warm as I know him to be, he used, I am persuaded, to Frank language unusually severe. He produced the pistols which he had provided, and they soon found out this spot. – It was Frank's chance to fire first; his ball struck on the breast of his antagonist: he rose, however, instantly, and discharged his piece; happily it failed, and the pistols having been heard in the house, the people, who now interposed, sent for a surgeon and conveyed the young man to bed. With some pain the ball was extracted, and all is safe; a slight wound only remains.'

I could retain my impatience no longer, and interrupted Burell – 'But this antagonist, this avenger of my wrongs, who is he, Burell? Tell me from what motive' –

'Motive!' repeated Burell, as he fixed his eyes on me: 'the man who has once seen Miss Morven, who in that once had an opportunity of beholding and form-ing an idea of her perfections, can he want a motive? Think then of such a man, and that ardent and ungovernable being will be presented before you.'

As he said this, what he had before uttered, joined to his own emotion, rushed with equal conviction upon my mind. Then it was that I feared, that I hoped, I wished, and yet dreaded to hear this name: then it was that my mind foreboded that it was his brother: I then ventured to flatter myself that the interest which from the first instant I had taken in him, was not unreturned. The pleasing imag-ination glided with the rapidity of light though my fancy, it seemed to recall my powers. 'Surely,' said I, with impetuosity, 'it cannot be – it is not' – I felt my error, and checked myself – I beheld Burell's countenance, and the glow which in a moment had seemed to reanimate me, the blush of expectation and of pleasure, almost of rapture, faded from my cheek. In a low voice he satisfied my doubts; he told my aunt it *was* his brother – that he had seen him, and there was nothing to apprehend. The surgeon had been sent for from Bath, none of eminence being nearer, and the whole town is acquainted with the affair, with numberless added inconsistencies.

Burell was incapable of further explanation; it was with visible pain he had gone thus far. He hastily took his leave, and was returning, he said, to attend on his brother. My aunt intreated, and he promised to see her again soon, – I was happy to escape from the importunate enquiries and surmises of that too tender woman. – I have not since sought any society. In tears and prayers for the peace of Burell, I will own it, for the safety of his brother, I have poured forth my soul to heaven, and I have opened it to you. How slowly approaches the time when I shall again converse with you! and till that period arrives, why is it that

> "Fancy augments the dangers of the deep,
> And expectation loads the wing of time"?[12]

The ardor with which I wish for your arrival, is equal to the affection which I have ever felt, which, still mingling with all other attachments, I ever must feel, in all its strength, for you, my beloved brother.

I am surprized at the length of my last letters, and you perhaps may never receive them, or, should they reach your hands, they may but little interest you.

– But no, I will not believe it. The narrative of those sentiments and emotions which arise in the heart – and, conscious of it as I am, why should I not say it? – the sensible heart of your sister, you are incapable of perusing with indifference; you will take part in every sensation of her soul, and, if you cannot be blind to its errors, you will, at least, behold them with the unreproaching pity of sympathy, and the tender partiality of affection.

––––––––

LETTER XL.

TWO days have passed, and I have not seen Burell; yet twice every day has he sent to my aunt an account of his brother's health: he has continued to mend, and now quits his apartment.

Why, my dear brother, is it, that, when I think on the rash action of this young man, I behold it with horror and detestation; yet, as the remembrance of it arises, I am not less partial to him – I am not less willing to imagine him possessed of all the virtues which my fancy has bestowed on him? Alas! my heart but too willingly excuses that warmth and impetuosity which it participates! I forget his crime, and behold him only wounded and bleeding for me, to whom he owes nothing, and of whose involuntary regard he is even unconscious. A thousand times have I recalled the words of his brother, 'He loves you to distraction; he is deserving of you.'

Generous Burell! I know what in these words he meant to convey. I admire in him this testimony to the merits of his rival; I feel a new and uncommon sensation in the certainty with which this expression should inspire me. Our hearts have beat in secret, but they have also beat in unison. I dwell on the idea, it seems to revive and reanimate me; yet I am not easy. Burell has discovered the dearest secret of my soul: I have myself acknowledged it to him. Perhaps, at the moment of first seeing Vincent with him, I was betrayed by the emotion I was then unable to conceal, as well as by that which succeeded, when he called for my confidence, and, overcome by that, all precaution was forgotten. As I recollect the avowal I myself made, I now tremble, lest, in seeking to render me happy, Burell should betray that secret to his brother. This reflection troubles me; yet, notwithstanding, I feel myself more easy, more chearful, more alive, than I have long been. My dear aunt, to whose affection and tenderness I owe so much, sees it and rejoices.

Ruth is charmingly recovered. I broke, in the most gentle manner, the whole to her. It is well over, and she knows my whole heart, and would chace from thence all doubt and uneasiness. She is anxious to see Vincent, and bids me look forward and be happy.

LETTER XLI.

I HAVE received a note from Burell. Fortunately I was alone at the moment of its arrival. A thousand times I have perused and pressed it to my heart, which beats with violence against its folds. I perceive and I blush at my own folly. To-morrow Vincent comes to ask and obtain my pardon for his rashness.

Ah! generous Burell, noble and delicate lover, you know my heart, yet can resolve to bring this intruder, this stranger, with whose power you are not unacquainted – Oh! lover deserving of that name, since it is my happiness alone that you wish. When I think of you, I shrink from my own littleness; I contemplate your actions with sensations which are only to be felt, and shed over them the truest tears of admiration.

LETTER XLII.

THE departure of the last star of the night, the bright rays of the morning, how welcome are they to my eyes! In this night which precedes a meeting so dear, so interesting, it was in vain that I courted repose. I have arisen; my window faces the east, and I have watched "the grey dawn and the pleiades"[13] in their progress. When I fixed my eyes on the majestic concave which overshadows me, even those sensations, which had so agitated me, disappeared; thanksgiving and reverence filled my heart.

Lives there, my brother, that blind and insensible being, who, beholding these miraculous works of Omniscience, could doubt their originating from divinity, their proceeding from the hands of an eternal and almighty Creator? Can such dreadful and impious absurdity enter the mind of the lords of this world, my dear brother? I never did, never can I believe it. There exists not, in the breast of man, that heart so cold, so dead, so irrational. It is not in nature to give birth to this living, yet impenetrable rock. Surely, in me, my brother, not to behold this morning rise, had been even a sin. Never may I forget to pour forth, at the footstool of mercy everlasting, of beneficence eternal, my prayers of gratitude! It is now three years only, since on this morning I awakened to the pure light of uncontaminated religion, and was released from the gloomy and impenetrable walls of superstition[14]: then it was that I sunk at the feet of you, my brother, my friend, my deliverer! Nature and genius had ever been dear to me: from that moment I was permitted to behold them, I received their divine influence into my soul; I pursued the flowery and delightful paths of science, paths from which I had feared to be for ever excluded. To heaven and to you it is that I owe this sacred and rapturous reflection, and never shall this morning escape me without my remembering and acknowledging it.

LETTER XLIII.

I HAVE begun another sheet; for I would not mingle ideas less sacred with those with which my bosom this morning overflowed. My hands, as they have ever on this day, have decked a little fantastical shrine, surrounded with every object which may heighten, if possible, those tender and grateful emotions with which I ever reflect on you. Your dear and faithful resemblance is placed in the midst. What is it I do not feel as I contemplate it?

Ruth has seen this little arrangement, and has attributed it to another cause; but, my brother, I can say, even at that moment, when hope and expectation beat high in my heart, this tribute is sincere, and is only yours: yet, I own it, my fingers at this minute, trembling, almost refuse their office; and this form, which has been flattered by your praises, is, to acknowledge my vanity, decorated as becomingly as possible. Ah! my brother, on this day, this hour perhaps, depends the whole happiness of my life. My agitation increases, and till I have seen him, I can write no more.

LETTER XLIV.

THIS day, the first and fairest of my existence, is past; the tumult of my spirits is subsided. What, my brother, are the flights of imagination to the feelings of the heart? I doubt no longer – my happiness is compleat – I have been introduced to Vincent – I beheld him elegant and animated, his eyes fixed only on your Theresa. When I entered the room, and my aunt introduced him to me with the words, how little necessary! 'My dear Theresa, when I present this gentleman to you as Mr. Vincent Burell, you will know all the thanks which are due from us to him,' trembling and hesitating, I was at a loss for expression, and, for the first time in my life, wished to testify gratitude inferior to that which I really felt – I was, for the first time, on my guard against that warmth of expression which has so often been blamed in me, but which I have not yet learnt to lament. Something, however, covered with a deep blush, I uttered. The confusion which glowed in his own fine features assisted to dispel mine. 'I have been informed,' said he, 'of Miss Morven's sentiments: they are those of humanity and of justice – but I have had the misfortune to act contrary to them; and I have now only to hope the transaction will be buried in oblivion, which she already has taught me to regret.' My aunt said all which politeness required, whilst I insensibly recovered myself; and two hours, the shortest surely of my life, were elapsed, before Vincent rose to take his leave. My aunt was not sparing of her compliments to him, and he answered them by addressing himself to me. He touched the keys of the instrument as he passed – It was not yet dinner-time, and my aunt, who loves to display the little perfections of her niece, bid me sit down to it. His soul is surely formed for music: the sound seemed to enter it, and, as he looked on me, every idea seemed lost in attention. – As I finished, I caught the gratifying words which passed from his lips, and spoke in the beams of his sparkling eyes. He looked at his watch – 'An hour, an instant!' said he, as he rose to take his leave. My heart sunk as the door shut after him. I flung myself on my aunt's bosom, and to her owned every past and every present emotion of my soul. I had then the satisfaction of doing justice to the whole conduct of S——. She heard me with affection and indulgence. Half my story was already known to her. She had learnt from his brother that I had met young Burell, that he was attached to me. That generous man had already smoothed the path of happiness for me; yet, selfish as I am, I have neglected to write of him. I have not yet told you, that, before I went to make my acknowledgements to Vincent, I had parted with him. I was just entering the room as Burell met me; and, leading me aside, accosted me: 'Charming emotion, beautiful angel,' he said, as I gave him my hand, into which he put a little packet; and then said, 'If you would see me tolerably composed, speak not; I have done all that friendship requires. I thought to have said, but I find myself incapable of it: I am now going to Italy; I will not stay even to see your brother. Theresa, remember me to him. Vincent, I repeat, adores you; but I have kept your secret – you are worthy of each other. Be his, be happy. As for me – time perhaps – But I move you – Adieu, dear woman! think of me sometimes.'

He hastily kissed the tear that had fallen on my cheek; he caught each of my hands, cast his eyes up, and pressed them to his heart.

'Theresa,' said he, 'may God restore to you your health! Live, beloved woman, for my brother, for your Vincent.'

He let my hands fall, and hurried out of the apartment. I attempted to speak; he heard my voice, and stopping for a moment a sigh reached him too deep to be stifled, and was gone. I then saw Vincent, and even this scene disappeared from my mind. –

I have perused the packet which Burell left with me; it explains the cause of Vincent's retirement. My aunt tells me you know the whole scheme. Ah, my brother, it is now no time to be angry. It contains also a letter, how dear and invaluable! from Vincent. In that letter I find a description of your Theresa, but so flattering a one, that only the first sensations of love could have prompted it.

In two days we quit Bath; we set forward on an excursion toward the sea, from whence we may now so soon hope to receive you, and I have persuaded Ruth to accompany us with her Sophy.

Adieu, my dear brother. Sleep presses heavy on my eye-lids, which have closed very little for some nights past. – Adieu.

Did I tell you Vincent was here again in the evening, and that my aunt is already attached to him? Or that she will not allow him to be like you? If I did, you will excuse the repetition of what is so near my heart, and you will yet believe me that affectionate sister of which you are more than deserving. – Adieu.

LETTER XLV.

SEVERAL days have passed, during which I have not written a word. My aunt has been somewhat indisposed, but I do not offer that as my excuse: the truth is, since Vincent has been permitted to come abroad, he has been here incessantly. – Oh, he is every thing that can justify the warmest partiality of an enthusiastic heart, and I find no difficulty before me but that of concealing a passion too ardent perhaps to be properly understood by any thing bearing the name of man.

We should have before this quitted Bath, had my aunt's health permitted; and I should then have missed an unexpected visit this morning, received from a character which interests and afflicts me.

Vincent was reading a new publication to my aunt and me, The Progress of Fashion.[15] The title is light, but the work is solid; and there is a strength in the whole of it that strikes me. The author by some, I know, is accused of displaying his learning; to me he seems only to be possessed of, and to make use of it. When we meet I will point out some passages that pleased me. Twice did Vincent lay down the book, and anticipate the remark which was just risen to my lips. It is true, we are formed for each other. –

But I forget this visitor who interrupted us. You may remember, perhaps, Mr. Manville, the curate whom I heard during my stay at Ruth's. It was he – his child, whose sickness is now almost beyond hope, has been sent here, as the last resource, to try the bath.[16] He introduced himself with some flattering expressions to me, but I have learnt how to estimate them. The error of his character has shocked me; but I could not behold him without reverence. He talked of the desperate state, of his beloved son with the expressions of meek and patient piety, worthy of a minister of the Gospel of Christ; but turn to another subject, and this divine part of his character disappears – Ruth was not present at his entrance, but he knew her to be with us, and his insatiable curiosity formed a

96 *The Victim of Fancy*

thousand surmises concerning the cause of her quitting —. I gave into none of them. At length, he said, she appeared to him a simple, inoffensive being – and it was cruel of Miss Morven to rob her of the only lover she had ever gained. This was coming too near the point. I was hurt, and said, with some indignation, 'You are yet, sir, mistaken, if you believe Mr. Hyde not to be devoted at present to Mrs. Aylesby.' He seemed chagrined; but Ruth then entering, he rose to congratulate her on her amended looks; and setting Sophy to point out the keys on the organ to him, 'Mrs. Aylesby,' he said turning to my aunt, 'has recovered that spirit and vivacity which used to distinguish her' – whilst the very bow which accompanied this compliment had irony in it. The sense which he possesses seems really to blind him, or he could not imagine that any one would see him contradict the sentiments he had expressed but an instant before, without discovering the hypocrisy of which he is thus for ever guilty, and internally despising him for it. He seems to feel the superiority of his own understanding so much, that he leaves any the least glimmerings of it in those who converse with him out of his account, and thus exposes himself most at the moment in which he levels his ridicule at others. – He entered into conversation with Vincent, and discovered learning equal to the talents I have before admired in him: he seemed, I thought, as if fathoming those of Vincent, and evinced more spleen than satisfaction, when assured they were not wanting.

When he rose to take his leave, he clasped my hand with the affection of a father, and, as I expressed my wishes for the recovery of his child, the tears of parental anxiety glistened in his eyes, and whilst the fire of true devotion seemed to kindle there, with the sanctity of a divine, he said, 'My good child, when you are old like me, you will know that the ways of God are inscrutable as just; but we must remember that to submit to his will with resignation is the only way man has of proving his belief in his word.'

Ah! my dear brother, was this man always what at that minute he appeared, he might alone reform the world; meek, pious, humble, beneficent, with talents to engage the affections, with manners to secure them; yet, blind and unhappy as he is, capable of rendering himself beloved, almost adored by all who knew him, he neglects those enviable advantages. He is heard and admired; but he is known, and must be despised. I beheld him with pity, and wept over that littleness of soul, that mean, unworthy duplicity which disgraces a character so capable of being all that is noble in nature, all that is respectable in religion.

His character struck Vincent, and he understood the drops I could not refrain shedding when he quitted us. My dear Ruth is more tranquil: She does not admire him like me, and she sees the errors I lament in him with detestation more than equal to her pity. There is, I remember, a sentiment in an author of very high repute, which comes home to this prevailing foible of his; and, though I do not wholly agree with it, I yet find it too applicable for me to forbear quoting it – "Those snarling, and satirical tempers, says he, every cut of whose tongue is like the stab of a poniard, find the unworthy abuse they make of talents, so estimable when rightly applied, goes not unpunished: as they spare none, so none spare them; and, were they at the highest top of exaltation, the lowest mortal upon earth would think he had a right to fall upon them, and to rob them of the good qualities they otherwise have."[17]

LETTER XLVI.

TO-MORROW we leave this place, where I arrived with wishes so fantastical, and hopes so ill founded, even the idea which then so fully possessed every faculty of my mind has passed away like a shadow: I am to believe it an illusion of my fancy only; I am to suppose that work which so much enchanted me, to be the production of this Dr. Goethé. To speak the truth, my dear brother, my heart and imagination are at present so much otherwise engaged, I scarce care whose it is; but I must ever remember how near I was owing to it my introduction to Vincent Burell.

I have been with my aunt to take leave of Dr. C—. He says that my health is perhaps mending, but that I yet think myself much better than I am. He complimented me on the recovery of my spirits: he knew the occasion of my coming to Bath, and has heard something also of the deception Frank had put on me, and in delicacy avoided his usual topic Werter – 'I saw it, and, Fear not, my good sir,' said I, 'this Werteromania is cured, and I could now almost hear you doubt of his excellence with patience.' – 'The object of your admiration,' said Dr. C—, rather archly, 'is perhaps less visionary at present, and something more easy to be pointed out and procured.' – I gave him no answer, if my confusion was not a sufficient one.

His daughter is married; I paid her my compliments, and we then quitted them, and went round a little circle of acquaintances my aunt had here renewed and contracted.

On our arrival at home we found Vincent; he was putting the last strokes to a drawing of mine. But I see that when I am with him he does nothing – could I wish him to do any thing but attend to me?

This is the last time that I shall write to you. Shall I confess the truth? I see I shall have no time to spare to my pen; but, my heart beating with the fondest affection, I am now hasting to meet you – to clasp my beloved brother – to present to him the permitted object of my affections – to taste, in their mutual conversations and endearments, all that the world can bestow – that elegant and durable felicity which is the offspring only of true sensibility of soul, of delicacy and refinement.

THERESA MORVEN.

The following narrative, which connects those letters which have preceded with those which conclude this volume, was gathered from the lips of Mrs. Aylesby, whose memory retained every transaction with the minuteness arising from the fixed and tender attachment to her friend Theresa Morven.

MISS MORVEN, with her aunt, her friend Ruth, and her lover, sat out to anticipate her meeting with her brother, full of those hopes which her sanguine disposition was so apt to give way to. To these friends, however, her precarious state of health was but too visible. The warmth and ardor of her heart supported her spirits, but her strength visibly decayed, her form wasted, and the bloom of youth and beauty faded from her cheek. But the expectation of her every wish being gratified by the return of her brother, and the unbounded affection of Vincent, (whose passion was as ardent as it was sudden,) gave hopes to her aunt, that, at a period when all the powers of nature are in their full force, she would recover the shock her constitution had sustained. It was an additional pang to her that it had been incurred by her dutiful attention. In that sickness, which Theresa mentions in the former part of her letters, this affectionate niece had watched, without rest or remission, for fifteen days and nights, at the bed of her aunt; and it was after being thus exhausted, that the malignancy had entered her blood, and attacked with violence a frame as remarkably delicate as beautiful in its construction. By the art of a skilful physician she escaped present death; but from that period, to the fond eyes of her aunt, her dissolution had seemed insensibly approaching. It is well known that great tenderness will make us fear, as well as hope, too much for its object; and Ruth, who had not seen Theresa in her full bloom, was willing to believe this only was the present case.

They travelled by easy stages to Portsmouth[19]; and even Mrs. Carlton saw a visible amendment in her niece. Here in impatient expectation they remained some days; – at length the hour so ardently expected by Theresa arrived. During the night a sloop from Gibraltar had entered the harbour; many soldiers were conveyed in it. The inhabitants of the town, warmed by that admiration of valour which the soul involuntarily owns, ran eagerly out to bind on the brows of their gallant defenders those laurel wreaths which they prepared as the reward of their virtue. Then from many a veteran, who had beheld unmoved the threats of approaching famine, and the more certain peril of the sword, dropped the noble tears of a brave and manly heart; and those souls, so undaunted in danger, now melted at this glorious testimony bestowed by the hands of their country – this most flattering memorial of fame which a soldier could ever receive. It is impossible to pass over this real and moving transaction, without quoting the glowing lines of the gallant Ercilla, on a subject so nearly similar, and which may with truth be applied, when the great expectations which were formed from the success of the enemies floating batteries is remembered.

> "These, by their efforts in the dread debate,
> Forced the determined will of adverse fate,
> From shouting triumph rushed the palm to tear,
> And fixed it on the brow of faint Despair."[21]

Theresa was just risen when their arrival and entrance was announced. Her servant enquired of one of them if Major Morven was in the vessel which brought them: he was answered in the affirmative. Theresa, in all whose emotions the truest devotion was ever mingled, threw herself in an extasy on her knees to heaven for his safe arrival. 'Ah! my brother,' she exclaimed, 'the moment with which I have so long flattered myself is at length arrived; my hands shall fix on your temples the laurel you have won, and you shall at once receive the invaluable meed[22] of fame and of affection.'

Her brother had not yet quitted the ship, and her aunt yielded to her eager desire of meeting him. Theresa, the tears streaming from her fine eyes, flew to the key. Lost in observing her, without a hat Vincent accompanied her, whilst her aunt and Ruth walked with less agitation behind. She saw the ship drawn close up to the shore, every one crowding round it. She was incapable of making any enquiry, but thought she perceived her brother detained from her on the deck. She sprung forward. A band of music had been playing to welcome the remaining passengers: it stopped on a sudden – a sick officer, borne by several soldiers, was conveying on shore, extended on a litter, pale, emaciated, and heedless even of the voice of fame. Theresa cast a pitying eye on him – she started – her whole frame was convulsed; she beheld in him that brother so ardently expected, so dearly beloved: she gave a faint scream –

> "From her slack hand the garland she had wreath'd
> Down dropt – and all its faded honours shed:
> Speechless she stood and pale!" – [23]

Conviction struck on her mind, and she fell senseless at the feet of those who supported him. Vincent shuddered as he comprehended the whole, and, catching her in his arms, ordered the supporters of the major to follow him. The faint voice of his sister had reached his ears; he attempted to rise, and saw her, like a corpse, conveying before him, and again with a deep groan concealed his head in the pillow.

Almost sinking beneath the shock, her aunt and Mrs. Aylesby joined the mournful procession. They arrived at their inn, and young Morven was laid on a bed, and assistance being sent for, Theresa soon recovered. Deaf to the entreaties of Vincent, she flew to her brother: at the sound of her voice, he made an effort, and, advancing a few steps, extended his arms to receive her. She flung her own round him, and, in a voice smothered with sobs, uttered, 'My brother! my beloved brother!' and they sunk together. Burell flew to support them. 'My dear Theresa,' in a low voice, said the major, 'fear nothing; think, my sister, of yourself, and I shall recover; I am already better.' – 'Better! alas! my brother, the hand of death is already on you. You are gone, you have forgotten your Theresa! I feel it plainly; my heart is already bursting. Oh! my brother – '

As she said this, she again fainted: her wandering words had flung the major into a dangerous agony: in this interval of total insensibility, Theresa was removed from him. Other assistance was called in; they were kept for some hours from each other – she revived, and the major was free from any immediate danger. –

In this interval it was thought adviseable to flatter Theresa into a belief that her brother was likely to recover; and unfortunately, in thus giving way to the present, they forgot to provide against the future: she was assured that every physician who had seen him had ascertained his safety. What she so earnestly wished, she learned to hope, and what she thought with reason she hoped, she at length believed. –

They saw one another again with less emotion; but remained together a few minutes only, since the major could not longer have sustained the exertions which in her presence gave him an appearance of amendment wholly foreign to what he felt. His health depended, he said, on her repose, and she was thus persuaded to quit him.

A draught was administered in her drink which might incline her to sleep. The major passed a tolerable night, and in the morning, making the following short recital to Vincent, divulged a secret which he had before carefully preserved from his sister, and to which his friend Burell hints in the two letters of his which appear. This was no other than his having received a dangerous wound at the moment of assisting the gallant Curtis[24] in the protection of his enemies. From this wound he was but just recovering, when he received that letter from his aunt, so alarming to an affectionate heart. He knew his sister, and delay, he thought, might be dangerous, as well as cruel. He opened his heart to a lady to whom he was then engaged. She joined in persuading him to set off instantly, and promised to wait for or soon follow him.

At this period he again became sensible of the attacks of a nervous fever, but he was silent concerning it; and the lady naturally enough attributed his lowness of spirits to his quitting her. – On the night previous to his departure, he sat up with her, and the wind rising suddenly in the morning, the captain of the vessel which was to convey him, without waiting for the major, availed himself of it – the vessel failed without him. When the major discovered this, he took a hasty leave of the woman he loved, and ventured in an open boat, in which, before he could overtake the sloop, he was tossed about for an hour in a rough sea, and exposed to a deluge of rain, which fell during the whole time. His health before ill established, the consequence was obvious: he was some days in a high delirium; there was no regular physician on board, and he was therefore improperly treated. The fever ceased at length, but its consequence remained; and when he arrived in England he was believed to be past the reach of all art.

This declaration was a dreadful stroke to his friends and those of Theresa; they foresaw and dreaded the effects it would have on her. For three days, however, they continued to deceive her; Vincent alone, who never quitted her side, had strength of mind sufficient to give her a hint of her brother's danger – but she had at first been flattered by them, and she had now learned to flatter herself. On the morning of the fourth, it was but too evident the whole must be soon known to her: the major's last hour was visibly approaching; a thousand sensations assured him of its certainty. Never, in the presence of Theresa, had one complaint escaped him; she had hoped, she believed, she even expected his recovery. He had felt a thousand tortures for the amiable woman he had left behind, but anxiety for Theresa now occupied every emotion of his heart: he saw her present before him; he beheld in her eyes, in the earnestness of that attention which she paid to him, how nearly her being was connected with his own. No other affection had weakened that she had ever so ardently acknowledged for him. At the approaching moment of his dissolution, he represented to himself all the agonies she would undergo, and thought only of relieving them. He fixed his eyes earnestly upon her, and, taking a silent and inward farewel of this tender and beloved sister of his soul, concealed the dreadful struggles which the resolution he at that moment fixed on cost him – that struggle of all the affections, which, lingering to the last round the yet sensible hearts of the children of mortality, oblige them to regret that world which has so frequently wounded them.

Sensible of his approaching end, he found a moment to advise to Vincent the administering of an opiate to Theresa: it was mingled with her sustenance, and he waited with a dreadful eagerness for the moment in which its operation should begin! Unasked, she took her harp, which he always loved to hear her touch, and drew from it a few of those soft and melting notes in which her sensible soul delighted. She stood opposite him; she fixed her eyes on him, unconscious of the drowsiness which began to weigh down their beautiful lids, and, in a low voice faltering with expressive sensibility, accompanied it with these words of her own, as they occurred to her:

"Ye blossoms of nature, ye dews of the morn,
   Which once I beheld with delight;
Ye planets which glitter, with radiance unshorn,
   Thro' the dark-bosom'd chaos of night:

No longer your beauties with rapture I see,
   Or catch the soft breath of the west:
Ah, what are your beauties, your fragrance to me,
   By my Henry no longer possess'd!

O Power Almighty, Dispenser of Good,
   Whom trembling and frail we adore,
Might health but revisit and glide thro' his blood,
   I could die and petition no more."[25]

She had scarce pronounced the last stanza, when she sunk into a slumber of which she knew not the cause. As she was moving away, a universal convulsion seized the frame of her brother; and all which he had felt burst at once in a deep and dreadful groan from his bosom: he seemed no longer sensible; the last paleness of death hung on his distorted and agonized brows. But that sound, which, from the acuteness of his emotion, had been little less than the expression of frenzy, roused Theresa from her beginning lethargy: she perceived herself conducted from his chamber, and a confused remembrance of her involuntary slumber recurred to her; the sound which had awakened her, every thing seemed to speak the most dreadful tidings. She saw the consternation of those who surrounded her, of Vincent, who supported her, eager, doubting, trembling. Nature made an effort; all her powers returned. She sprung from them – she rushed to the chamber of death – she gazed earnestly on her brother – she pronounced his name – wan, distorted, agonized, he answered not. She clasped him in her arms; she pressed him to her foreboding bosom – he opened his eyes, already overspread with the dimness of death, and fixed them yet expressive of tenderness on her. 'Hereafter, my dear Theresa,' inwardly he said – 'hereafter' – No tears wetted her pale and desolate cheek, but his words seemed to sink into her soul. He made another effort, the last of which expiring nature was capable: he drew her nearer to him, whilst his eyes, intently fixed upward, marked the fervor he yet felt. 'Father of Being, thou who gavest, thou who shalt now receive the breath of my existence – assist, support – if it be thy will, hasten the moment when with thee we shall rejoice for ever.' She continued to hold him in her arms; she felt the last pulsation of his heart, the last sigh from his lips breathed on her cheek. All which she underwent operating with the opiate she had taken, without closing her eyes, every faculty seemed suspended; she appeared totally insensible. As she had thrown her arms round him, she had locked her fingers, and no persuasions could make her alter their position: force was at length used; her delicate frame felt the injury. She seemed a little roused, and something like recollection dawn'd upon her as they removed her from him; but after putting her hand on her heart, it fell listless and unconscious by her side. For two days she continued in this state, but on the third night a deep and heavy sleep fell on her; it was a flattering symptom, but a few hours put an end to it. Waking, she recollected, she lamented, in terms the most pathetic, her absence from her brother, and talked of his loss.

Vincent could no longer bear to remain near her. Half distracted, he tore himself from her, and mourned over the loss of all his hopes. Her senses were but imperfectly returned; they only pointed out to her the object of her lamentation, and the extent of her misery. Her aunt and Vincent, whose anxiety almost bordered on frenzy, were not recognized by her – they, who had been witnesses, who had participated so greatly in all she had felt. All hopes of restoring her were lost, and her aunt, whose health was at all times but in-different, affected beyond recovery by the double shock, quickly followed young Morven to the grave.

Miserable as Vincent was, he yet put the affairs of the Major in a proper train; and at the same time wrote to the friends of the lady to whom he had been engaged, and transmitted to them her picture which was taken from his neck when dead, and inclosed it with a few lines which he had dictated before his death, and a lock of his hair.

Mrs. Aylesby never quitted Theresa, but with her Sophy would weep over and vainly attempt to soothe her. Sometimes when the little innocent flung itself on Theresa's neck, and deluged her with her tears, she would weep and gaze on her, but remain otherwise insensible: it awakened a little, however, her attention, and was therefore imagined to be of service. At other times, she would remain for hours resting on her harp only, now and then touching a string; her look cast with a wild and melancholy earnestness towards heaven, her hair falling neglected over her beautiful shoulders, whilst only the deep sighs which at intervals escaped her bosom, shewed any recollection.

In these moments, Vincent, at length become more inured to misery, would fling himself at her feet, and in words the most pathetic conjure her to answer him, to look at him: he would press the emaciated hand which hung by her side, and for a moment attract her eyes; but their rays were again quenched in insensibility, and, again leaning her head against her harp, whilst her tears fell silently on her bosom, her forlorn look of dejection returned.

One evening, however, when he had sat for hours looking at, and sometimes speaking to her, he thought at length that she seemed to awaken, and to move. He spoke again, 'If you have any comprehension, answer me, my beloved Theresa,' She pressed her hand on her heart, and looked at him with attention; and then, shaking her head, said, in a faint voice, but ever unalterably sweet and tender, 'Alas! I remember nothing – whoever you are, I know you not.'

Those words, dreadful as they were, were grateful: she spoke, she was at last roused, and hope sprung up in his breast. He sent immediately for her physician; an alteration was approaching. She was attacked with a fever, and it was not thought possible she should recover; but unexpectedly she sustained it; in a few days it was subdued, and her clearer perceptions returned. She remembered her misfortune, but she wept over it: she heard of the loss of her aunt, and bore it without relapsing.

By her attendance on her friend, the health of Ruth was injured; and Theresa, who had been removed during her state of insensibility to her house, perceived it with concern. Her solicitude for the ease of others attended her to the verge of the grave: she formed an idea of relieving Ruth, by having herself conveyed to the house where she first saw the younger Burell. His attachment was yet dear to her, and supported, though it was incapable of restoring her. He would sit for hours in silence, mingling his tears with hers. Accompanied by her maid, who was much attached to her, thither she determined to go.

Ruth gave into this whim, and suffered her to depart, at the same time resolving to follow her; but the illness of her child, who unexpectedly sickened with the small-pox, prevented her. The heart of Theresa foreboded they should meet no more: she pressed her in a last feeble embrace; she dropped a tear of resignation on her cheek, and was conveyed away. The child, whose little affections had flown out so warmly to her, was prevented with difficulty from running after her. Theresa, at the last turning of the road, where it was possible to behold the little habitation, raised herself up: she saw the handkerchief of Ruth, and with her white hand waved to her a last farewel.

At Bath Vincent met with the young ensign Villers and his sister, and the latter, deeply affected, as a tribute of gratitude, earnestly intreated to be permitted to return with Miss Morven to the apartments she had now quitted, to watch over and tend her. Theresa heard and willingly granted this request. From that hour Joannah fulfilled to her every office of tenderness which a heart gentle and grateful could suggest. Theresa at length arrived at the end of her journey; and the following letters, which conclude her story, are all dated from the little retired lodgings where she first saw Vincent.

LETTER XLVII.

THERESA MORVEN *to Mrs.* AYLESBY.

I AM arrived at this spot, and am nearly in the same state in which I left you, perhaps a little weaker. –

O my Ruth, I had fancied that I could write to you; but I am incapable. When I attempted to sit up without support, a universal tremor and faintness seized me, the pen dropped from my fingers, and you will be indebted to Joannah for all my future letters. Sustained by the trembling arm and unremitting attention of Vincent, I am just capable of dictating.

My dear Ruth, when I recollect all the past, I am yet thankful. When I remember that the sun has arisen, and I beheld not his beams, that he has set, and I was unconscious of their departure, I rejoice that I am again able to address my Maker, to receive comfort from his divine promises. I shall not, my dear Ruth, depart insensible of his mercies.

How vain are the imagination of man's heart! I thought to meet my brother, and then my happiness would be complete. I did meet him – but, alas! this remembrance, how dreadful! disorders me. – Dear shade! if, released from the weaknesses of mortality, thou yet hoverest round the languid head of thy Theresa, O mark to her the period of her existence, the moment when she shall rejoin thee for ever.

LETTER XLVIII.

THE long, long night is past; the morning, whose breath has so often awakened me to pleasure, has risen. In short and interrupted slumbers I have beheld my brother. His mild countenance beamed with divine pity. He gathered his white robe from behind him; with his pale hand he beckoned to me, and disappeared. I am convinced of it, I shall follow and I shall meet him –

"Who was in life but as a dream to me;"[26]

and, freed from the repinings which yet press at my heart, I shall be happy.

My dear Ruth, this tenderest of human beings, this affectionate and delicate Vincent, is absent; and I own to you, when I behold him, when I see him cast his fine eyes to heaven in prayer for me, when I mark the melancholy that overshadows and devours him, I feel a momentary repining; I look back upon the world, and think I could yet remain there. There was a time, my Ruth, that I should have repined at being one of those, who depart unknown to the world – whose names, consigned to oblivion,

— "Without or infamy or fame,
Close the blank business of this mortal scene."[27]

But those moments of vanity, if such they were, are past. Frail and inconsistent as I am, I trust that the errors incident to my nature, will meet with pity from the God of Mercy. I endeavour at resignation, I listen to his holy and immutable word, and experience it. I remember the raptures which I felt at my release from confinement; as an error, I lament over those energies which have destroyed me. I now reflect, almost with envy, on the tranquillity of those whom no feelings awaken from the long calm of life, whose days glide away ever the same, and ever undisturbed. But I was not born to be one of them ********

Supported by Vincent, and the amiable girl who now writes to you, I have been conducted into the little garden. I stopped at the door where I first saw Vincent approaching me, and a tear fell on his shoulder as I recollected the emotions I then first experienced. We were silent, but I saw all his anguish, and would have given the world to conceal my own. When we arrived at the low wall which bounds the garden, I rested on a couch already placed there for me. Vincent attempted to smother his emotion, but he was capable only of hurrying from me to conceal it. The soft breath of the western wind, which revived all nature around, run with a cold and deadly shivering to my heart – I could not help recalling to mind those beautiful and natural lines of Michael Bruce[28], so applicable to the situation of your faded Theresa.

> "Starting and shiv'ring in the inconstant wind,
>   Meagre and pale, the ghost of what I was;
> Beneath some blasted tree I lie reclin'd,
>   And count the silent moments as they pass:
>
> The winged moments, whose unstaying speed
>   No art can stop or in their course arrest;
> Whose flight shall shortly count me with the dead,
>   And lay me down in peace with them that rest."[29]

Vincent knows my passion for music: at some distance he touched a few stops on his flute; the sound overcame me – I was conveyed in doors, and the couch on which I now extend my feeble limbs, perhaps, I shall rise from no more.

LETTER XLIX.

HOW does the soul linger in this habitation of clay! the links which unite them are not yet broken within me. Shall the day be ever again beheld by these eyes? Surely it is impossible; something assures me I shall behold no more the blush of the morning sky, the still fragrance of the dews of evening.

My dear Ruth, with trembling yet steady hope I meet my end; I go to the house of darkness, but the time of that darkness will have a period, and we know it: "The morning *will* dawn on the night of the grave."[30] This fortitude which I feel, which inspires and animates me, why cannot I infuse it into the heart of Vincent, and of you, my dear Ruth?

I have performed the most sacred offices of religion, and feel myself placid and resigned: I can even look at Vincent; I can think of all which I lose in him, and lie down to close my eyes in the long and heavy slumber of the grave in peace.

* * * *

A severe fainting has attacked me: on recovering I found myself in the garden; when, at length, I opened my eyes, I beheld Vincent kneeling by my side, and concealing his face in the pillow. 'Vincent,' I said, and pressed my feeble hand on his shoulder, 'I am not yet departed.'

Ah! Ruth, why does he love me with this ardor which consumes him?

He started at the sound of my voice, uttered a thanksgiving, and he pressed his lips on my forehead.

O my friend! when the last, last damp of death shall be found there, how will he support it? I thought of that moment, which with rapid and certain steps I beheld approaching, and attempted to console him. 'My dear Vincent, in regretting me, you will pay a tribute which perhaps I deserve from you – but exert yourself; in a period, how short to the duration of eternity, we shall meet, we shall be happy. Resort to religion, Vincent, and even on this spot you will find consolations; you will remember that tender and virtuous passion which you have here inspired and participated; and the hand which I now press trembling in mine, shall close these eyes, which never beheld, which, had ages been added to my existence, never could have beheld with love any object but yourself.'

I had wished to say more to him, but the cold tremor of his hand made me fear for him. It is you then, my dear Ruth, who I must trust will comfort his agitated heart; it is to you that I must confide my last tender remembrances to his generous brother: tell him, in all the pangs I have endured, I have thought of him as he deserved: tell him he is united with Vincent in my last prayers to heaven. And, when capable of her mother's sensibility, tell my little Sophy the short story of your Theresa's life; from that let her learn to regulate the passions, even the most innocent of her heart: it is the impetuosity of mine, I am persuaded, which has done much in destroying me. Mark to her, my dear Ruth, the disappointment to which all earthly expectations are liable, even at the moment when we look on their completion as certain. If we would live, we must regulate, we must even subdue the tenderest feelings of the human soul. You will enjoy, my dear Ruth, with her, with your Frank, the competency you deserve; and sometimes, when the revolving year brings back the remembrance of your first seeing Theresa, you will bestow a mutual sigh to the memory of the friend who loved you.

Farewel, my dear Ruth – confusion and darkness seem to seize on my intellects – I feel the tears of Vincent, but I see not the eyes from whence they flow;

a thick mist obscures my own. All will soon be over. I am to be laid at the side of the brother, for whom I lived, for whom I die.

LETTER L.

Vincent Burell, *to* Frederick Burell.

THE dreadful moment of certainty is come – it is past! –

> "The worm now tastes that rosy mouth,
> Where glow'd short time the smiles of youth;
>   And in my heart's dear home
> Her snowy bosom loves to lie."[31]

Yes, those pure lips where greater sweetness dwelt "than breath shut up from a new-folded rose,"[32] are closed and pale for ever. This purest spirit that ever inhabited a daughter of mortality, is fled. Such is the story you have to hear, and it is mine to relate it to you. It was midnight, and her senses had been some hours imperfect, when, on à sudden, she recollected me. Meek and patient to her last moments, she pressed my hand, cold almost as her own, to her lips, and as I bent over the departing angel, in a soft sigh of pity and resignation her gentle spirit returned to the bosom of him who gave it.

It is for colder hearts than mine to describe feelings; but I have seen the damp vault receive the beloved of my soul. I retain my being and wonder at it. To-morrow I embark to meet you. We will wander together, and once every year will we return to the scene made sacred by her residence and departure. I will point to you the spot where her tears have fallen; perhaps then the sources of mine may be opened, and we shall weep over it together.

Angel of light! – "of my lost youth, thou only bride!"[33] overshadow me with thy wings. Breathe that religion which thou recommendedst to me through my soul, and I may yet be resigned to the decrees of heaven.

Forgive me, my brother, as you feel for me. The moment of our meeting will be dreadful: arm yourself with fortitude to bear your own sorrows, and to soothe those of,

Your miserable brother,

Vincent Burell.

FINIS.

ENDNOTES

Volume I

1. *Author of the* CONQUESTS *of the* HEART: a reference to Tomlins's first novel *The Conquests of the Heart. A novel. By a young lady. In three volumes* (Dublin: printed for Price, S. Watson, Moncrieffe, Jenkin, Walker, *et al.*, 1785), a highly romanticized biography of a Jamaican friend ('R. N.'), the subject of two of Tomlins's poems, 'To R. N.' and 'To the same Friend'.

2. *With frames and constitutions weaker than Men have ... it absorbs all other considerations*: the epigraph is taken from *The Progress of Fashion: exhibiting a view of its influence in all the departments of life* (London: J. Sewell, 1786), pp. 73–4. Tomlins has altered and condensed the text down. The source-text reads: 'The great end of a human being relatively to his fellow-creatures is social happiness. In the union between man and wife, this is almost the sole object. And how shall we expect to attain this end, with a woman given entirely to any one pursuit of science of pleasure? If of science, there is surely little prospect of finding, combined with it, a steady attention to the duties of a wife, a mother, or a friend. The reason is obvious. With frames and constitutions weaker than we have, their passions are warmer, and the rays of their genius concentrate to the object on which they engage themselves more strongly than ours. It absorbs all other considerations. If of pleasure, the danger is greater, because its influence extends beyond the department of œconomy: it is not the arrangement of furniture, nor the disposition of the table, nor the regulation of the family alone, which suffers, but the fame, the fortune, and the happiness – But mark – this is the pleasure which becomes an occupation. It is that alone, which never fails in the end to degenerate into evil'. When quoted more fully various themes emerge from this source-text, to which Tomlins sought to respond: the dynamics between man and wife, domestic life, and the constitutions of women.

3. *Dedication. To William Hayley, Esq.*: William Hayley (1745–1820), a poet and biographer of note. *Triumphs of Temper* (London: J. Dodsley, 1781) has been widely touted as his most accomplished work. This allegorical poem in rhyming couplets sought to 'delineate the more engaging features of Female Excellence', p. ix. It influenced a number of women, most notably Emma Hamilton. Throughout *The Victim of Fancy* Tomlins makes numerous references to a number of Hayley's works.

4. *of Britain's living choir*: from the first epistle of Hayley's *An Essay on Epic Poetry; in five epistles to the Revd. Mr. Mason* (London: J. Dodsley, 1782): 'Say! MASON, Judge and Master of the Lyre! / Harmonious Chief of Britain's living Choir / Say! wilt Thou listen to his weaker strains, / Who pants to range round Fancy's rich domains', ll. 13–16. Hay-

ley's poem is addressed to William Mason (1725–97), a leading contemporary poet and garden designer. Although he experimented tirelessly with literary form, many critics have characterised Mason as conventional, overly pious, and a dull imitator of Milton and Thomas Gray. Nonetheless, his *Heroic Epistle to Sir William Chambers* (London: J. Almon, 1773) was one of the best-selling poems of the eighteenth century.

5.   *the female band*: various encomia to Hayley penned by prominent literary women, including Hannah More, Helen Maria Williams and Anna Seward, appeared in the 1780s. See Morchard Bishop, *Blake's Hayley: The Life, Works, and Friendships of William Hayley* (London: Victor Gollancz, 1951).

6.   *fair Comnena's shade*: Anna Komnene (latinized as Comnena) (1083–1153), a Byzantine princess often considered to be one of the first female historians in the Western world. Her *Alexiad* (*c.*1148) is an account of the reign of her father, the emperor Alexios I Komnenos (latinized as Alexius I Comnenus). See *Biographium Fæmineum. The female worthies: or, memoirs of the most illustrious ladies, of all ages and nations* (London: printed for S. Crowder, J. Payne, *et al.*, 1766), vol. 1, pp. 150–1. Hayley references Comnena in *An Essay on History; in three epistles to Edward Gibbon, Esq.* (London: J. Dodsley, 1780), l. 399.

7.   *'not an artist, yet a friend to art'*: from the fifth epistle of Hayley's *Essay on Epic Poetry*: 'If not an Artist yet a friend to Art', l. 420.

8.   *As those striking traits of originality and spirits ... given rise to the severest censure*: Goethe's *Die Leiden des Jungen Werthers* (1774) was translated into English as *The Sorrows of Werter: a German Story* (London: J. Dodsley, 1779) in two volumes, and reached more than half a dozen editions by 1786. See my Introduction for a fuller discussion of 'Werteromania'.

9.   *master of the lyre*: The Greek god Apollo. According to the most prominent version of the myth, the infant Hermes stole a number of Apollo's cows and took them to a cave in the woods near Pylos. Here he found a tortoise and killed it, then removed the insides. Using the shell of the tortoise and the intestines of a cow he fashioned the first lyre. Hermes then began to play music on the lyre. Apollo, a god of music, fell in love with the instrument and allowed Hermes to keep the cattle in exchange for it.

10.   *Gibraltar*: The 1713 Treaty of Utrecht awarded Britain sovereignty over Gibraltar. Various fortifications were soon established and occupied by British troops in the area dubbed '*the British Neutral Ground*'. During the American Revolution, the Spanish, who had sided against the British, imposed a stringent blockade against Gibraltar as part of an unsuccessful siege (the so-called Great Siege of Gibraltar) that lasted for more than three years, from 1779 to 1783. On 14 September 1782 the British destroyed the floating batteries of the French and Spanish besiegers and peace preliminaries were finally signed in February 1783. The final siege was frequently alluded to in eighteenth-century fiction, such as in Henry Fielding's *Amelia* (London: A. Millar, 1752) and the anonymous *Edward, a Novel* (London: T. Davies, 1774). Frederick Pilon also produced *The Siege of Gibraltar: a musical farce, in two acts* (London: G. Kearsly, 1780). The siege is also discussed by James Macpherson, author of the Ossian poems, in *The History of Great Britain, from the Restoration, to the Accession of the House of Hannover* (London: W. Strahan, and T. Cadell, 1775), and by a number of contemporary naval historians and travel writers. Catharine Upton wrote an epistolary account: *The Siege of Gibraltar, from the twelfth of April to the twenty-seventh of May, 1781. To which is prefixed, some account of the blockade* (London: printed for the authoress, and sold by J. Fielding, [1781]).

11.   *Vincent*: the later love-interest of the heroine, Vincent Burell, is introduced in the first letter, and indeed on the first page, of the novel. Here his brother Frederick describes him warmly as loyal, valorous and noble. Frederick refers to his own duties as an elder

brother, thereby establishing a prominent theme in the novel: the ethical and emotional dynamics of sibling relationships.

12. *her being charmed with a production ... who thinks this censure unjust, stands forth as a champion in his cause*: Frederick Burell's disparaging reference is to Goethe's inflammatory novella *Die Leiden des Jungen Werthers*, which had become immensely popular across Europe.

13. *I don't know how it is ... and whoever this author is, he has been misunderstood and abused*: Theresa is specifically referring to the anonymous translator of Goethe's novella into English. Her warm praise of the book is in stark contrast with Burell's letter to Morven.

14. *read Homer in the original*: although some middling class girls were taught and urged to read classical literature, most practically minded pedagogues recommended that they use modern translations. Greek and Latin were staples of a young gentleman's education.

15. *I admired their crapes and their blonds*: the fabric and colour of clothing, such as dress aprons. Crape is defined as 'a thin silk gauze, crimped' in C. Willett Cunningham and Phillis Cunnington, *Handbook of English Costume in the Eighteenth Century* (London: Faber and Faber, 1957), p. 417.

16. *the ashes of the divine* Milton: John Milton (1608–74), widely imitated poet and polemicist. In a poem written in 1795 Tomlins praises Milton, the 'matchless Bard! whose ever-during name / Thy Britain's pride, her wonder, and her joy', *Tributes of Affection: with The Slave; and other poems. By a lady; and her brother* (London: printed by H. and C. Baldwin; for T. N. Longman, Paternoster-Row; and C. Dilly, in the Poultry, 1797), p. 67.

17. *the grottos of Tivoli*: in the Lazio region of central Italy.

18. *the songs of Ossian*: Ossian is the narrator and supposed author of a cycle of poems which the Scottish poet James Macpherson claimed to have translated from ancient sources in the Scots Gaelic. Written in a sentimental style, the Ossianic works were immensely popular across Europe in the second half of the eighteenth century and inspired a number of adaptations and imitations. The protagonist of Goethe's *Werther* is himself an avid reader and translator of the songs.

19. *the nameless translator*: The 1779 translation of *Werther* into English has been variously attributed to Daniel Malthus and Richard Graves.

20. *my admiration of painting, that more than speaking sister of poetry*: it was common practice to refer to art, poetry and music as "sister arts". See the first epistle of Hayley's *Essay on Epic Poetry*, l.81.

21. *those relations who so obligingly wished to immure me for life*: that is, sent Theresa Morven to a nunnery.

22. *the British Raphael*: this sobriquet has been applied to a number of painters, most notably Sir Joshua Reynolds (1723–92), a major portrait and history painter and art theorist. Reynolds was a keen student of Raphael's works, especially the *School of Athens* and *Madonna della Sedia*.

23. *'Severe in youthful beauty'*: from Milton's *Paradise Lost*: 'So spake the Cherub; and his grave rebuke, / Severe in youthful beauty, added grace / Invincible: abash'd the Devil stood, / And felt how awful goodness is, and saw / Virtue in her shape how lovely; saw, and pin'd / His loss'. Milton's epic was widely printed throughout the century; this version of the text is taken from *Paradise Lost. A poem, in twelve books... A new edition, with notes of various authors, by Thomas Newton* (London: J. and R. Tonson and S. Draper, 1749), book IV, ll. 844–9.

24. *My aunt recommends history to me*: Hester Chapone, in *Letters on the Improvement of the Mind, addressed to a young lady* (London: printed by H. Hughs for J. Walter, 1773) recommends that young women read history, poetry (especially Shakespeare, Milton, Homer, Virgil), and moral philosophy. But as a caveat she insists that 'the greatest care should be taken in the choice of those *fictitious stories*, that so enchant the mind – most of which tend to inflame the passions of youth, whilst the chief purpose of education should be to moderate and restrain them', vol. 2, p. 144.

25. *postillion*: someone who rides the near horse of a pair in order to guide the horses pulling a carriage (especially a carriage without a coachman).

26. *the tears which I have shed for that dear and amiable woman ... resigned her own into the hands of her Creator*: evidently Theresa's mother died in childbirth.

27. *Surely she, whom my father once made his wife, injured as I was by her artifice, must be secure: her name shall not be mentioned by me with detestation*: an allusion to the wicked step-mother who interred her in the nunnery.

28. *His small estate died with him ... in the manner which you now see*: the property rights of daughters, wives and widows were limited by a number of provisions in British common law in the eighteenth century. See *Novel Relations: The Transformation of Kinship in English Literature and Culture, 1748–1818* (Cambridge: Cambridge University Press, 2004), pp. 38–76.

29. *Countess of Genlis*: Stéphanie-Félicité Ducrest de Genlis, often referred to as Madame de Genlis (1746–1830), a notable French writer and educator much admired in England.

30. *Pamela*: Genlis was the adoptive mother of two English girls, Pamela and Hermine. Although her parentage was the topic of salacious gossiping, Pamela later married Lord Edward Fitzgerald. See Introduction, *Adelaide and Theodore, or Letters on Education*, ed. Gillian Dow, Chawton House Library Series (London: Pickering & Chatto, 2007), pp. xv–xvi.

31. *the Benedicite read*: The Benedicite (also known as Benedicite Omnia Opera, or A Song of Creation) is a canticle – a hymn taken from the Bible – that may be used in the Anglican or Lutheran liturgy of Morning Prayer.

32. *Gibbon*: Edward Gibbon (1737–94), leading historian and man of letters. His most influential work remains *The History of the Decline and Fall of the Roman Empire* (London: W. Strahan, and T. Cadell, 1776–88).

33. *Hayley*: William Hayley (see note 3).

34. *Reynolds*: Sir Joshua Reynolds (see note 22).

35. *Copley*: John Singleton Copley (1738–1815), an American portrait and history painter and a friend of Reynolds. *The Defeat of the Floating Batteries at Gibraltar, September 1782* depicts the defeat of the floating French and Spanish batteries during the Great Siege of Gibraltar. The Governor of Gibraltar, General Eliott, is seated on horseback and gesturing towards the British rescue of the defeated Spanish sailors.

36. *a may-pole raised*: a tall wooden pole erected in celebration of May Day or Midsummer. With roots in Germanic paganism, maypole rituals, especially dancing, have been performed off and on in England since the sixteenth century.

37. *the swiftest was to be queen, and I had prepared a garland to crown her*: During maypole celebrations a May Queen is crowned. She wears a white gown to symbolize purity.

38. *a sprig of myrtle*: a flowering plant with white petals. It is often used to signify love and immortality. In Greek mythology myrtle is sacred to Aphrodite, goddess of love and beauty, and to Demeter, goddess of fertility. In Samuel Johnson's 'Verses, written at the request of a Gentleman to whom a Lady had given a sprig of Myrtle', the flower has

ambivalent connotations as a love token: 'The myrtle crowns the happy lovers heads, / The unhappy lovers graves the myrtle spreads', *The Poetical Works of Samuel Johnson* (London: G. Kearsley, 1785), p. 170.

39. *white narcissus*: Daffodils in English, and typically white and yellow in colour. It heralds the return of spring and yet in some cultures it is associated with death. It can also symbolise unrequited love and vanity.

40. *cowslips*: primula veris, usually yellow in colour. Also known as Paigle, Fairy Cups, Mayflower, and Key Flower. According to legend, St Peter dropped the keys to Heaven and Cowslips grew where they landed.

41. *violets*: The colours of viola range from violet through various shades of blue, yellow, white, and cream. In Christian art the violet represents humility and even timidity.

42. *sweetmeats*: a sweet delicacy prepared with sugar, honey, and the like.

43. *Behold an Israelite in whom there is no guile!*: 'Jesus saw Nathanael coming to him, and saith of him, Behold an Israelite indeed, in whom is no guile!' (John 1:47).

44. *about a league from Versailles*: about 3 miles or 4.8 km. The French *lieue* has variously been measured on a scale from 3.25 km to 4.68 km. As a unit of measurement here it refers to the distance a person or a horse can walk in an hour.

45. *a cavalcade*: a procession on horseback.

46. *the pump-room*: neoclassical salon located in the centre of Bath in the West of England. Since the late seventeenth century the hot Spa water has been a recognised treatment for certain ailments.

47. *the name of* Lee *circulated in a whisper*: Sophia Lee (1750–1824), novelist and playwright best known for her gothic and historical fiction. After the death of their father, Lee and her sisters settled in Bath. With the money earned from her first play, *The Chapter of Accidents* (London: T. Cadell, 1780), Lee financed a local girls' school.

48. Temeraire: téméraire (French): reckless, bold, daring. The equivalent English word is *temerity*, from the Latin *temeritas*, but the French is perhaps best translated here as 'the audacious one'.

49. *the writer of Cecilia*: Frances Burney (1752–1840), also known as Fanny Burney and, from 1793, as Madame d'Arblay. *Cecilia; or Memoirs of an Heiress* (London: T. Payne and Son, and T. Cadell, 1782), in five volumes, was her second novel. Burney and Lee were frequently compared with one another. See *Thraliana: The Diary of Mrs. Hester Lynch Thrale*, ed. Katharine C. Balderston (Oxford: Clarendon Press, 1942), vol. 2, p. 695. In 1786 William Godwin listed Lee and Burney together as famous people he wanted to meet. See W. St Clair, *The Godwins and The Shelleys: A Biography of a Family* (Baltimore, MD: The Johns Hopkins University Press, 1989), p. 38.

50. *I will read this* Recess: Sophia Lee's *The Recess, or, A Tale of Other Times* (London: T. Cadell, 1783–5), a three-volume epistolary novel exploring the conflict between Elizabeth I and Mary, Queen of Scots as told through the eyes of Mary's fictional daughters. Going into a second edition in 1786, it enjoyed immense popularity for many years and was translated into five languages, namely French, German, Spanish, Portuguese, and Swedish.

51. *Though with five hundred pounds a year, she bestows as if she had five thousand*: roughly £50,000 and £500,000 respectively in modern currency, as calculated based on relative purchasing power.

52. *whist*: a popular four-person card game in the eighteenth century. See Edmund Hoyle's *A Short Treatise on the Game of Whist* (London: John Watts, 1742).

53. *'O what a noble mind is here o'erthrown!'*: Ophelia's lament for the seemingly mad Prince Hamlet in Shakespeare's *Hamlet*, Act III, Scene I.

54. *the author of Evelina and Cecilia*: Frances Burney (see note 49). The three-volume *Evelina; or the History of a Young Lady's Entrance into the World* (London: T. Lowndes, 1779) was published anonymously in fear of angering her father, Dr Charles Burney, a respected musicologist and author. It was her first novel. In 1785 Tomlins's brother Thomas Edlyne Tomlins ('E') wrote a versified version of an extract from the third volume of *Evelina*: 'Lady Belmont to Sir John Belmont', *Tributes of Affection*, pp. 122-4.

55. *'all ear'... 'might create a soul under the ribs of death'*: from Milton's *Comus, a mask*: 'I was all Ear, / And took in Strains, that might create a Soul / Under the Ribs of Death – but O! ere long, / Too well I did perceive it was the Voice / Of my most honour'd Lady, your dear Sister'. This version of the text is taken from the widely reprinted *Comus, a Mask: (now adapted to the stage) as Alter'd from Milton's Mask at Ludlow-Castle, which was Never Represented but on Michaelmas-Day, 1634; before the Right Honble. the Earl of Bridgewater, Lord President of Wales* (London: printed by J. Hughs, for R. Dodsley, 1738), p. 35. The phrase 'all ear' also appears in Milton's *Paradise Lost*: 'when Adam first of men / To first of women Eve thus moving speech, / Turn'd him all ear to hear new utterance flow'. Richard Bentley noted that this 'pretty expression' resembles the Latin *Totum te cupias, Fabulle, nasum* (from Catullus). This is quoted in Thomas Newton's edition of *Paradise Lost: A Poem, in Twelve Books* (op. cit.), book IV, ll. 408–10.

56. *the Tempest*: a late Shakespeare play in which a tempest is raised by the banished sorcerer Prospero, the usurped Duke of Milan, thereby wrecking the ship of his enemies, which includes his brother Antonio.

57. *that beautiful and heart-rending poem of Falkner's, the Shipwreck*: a reference to William Falconer's *The Shipwreck. A Poem. In Three Cantos. By a Sailor* (London: A. Millar, 1762). A sixth edition appeared in 1785.

58. *'so winning, soft, so amiably mild'*: this appears to be an inversion of the lines in Milton's *Paradise Lost*: 'What could I do / But follow strait, invisibly thus led? / Till I espy'd thee, fair indeed and tall / Under a platan; yet methought less fair / Less winning soft, less amiably mild', book IV, ll. 475-9.

59. *two rubbers*: in the card game whist the term "rubber" refers to the series of games being played, whether the best of three or best of five, and so on.

60. *'Who feel, whene'er I touch the lyre, / My spirits sunk beneath my proud desire'*: a misquotation of William Hayley's 'For me, who feel, whene'er I touch the lyre, / My talents sink below my proud desire' in the fourth epistle of *An Essay on Epic Poetry*, ll. 413–14.

61. *the words of Caracchi*: Antonio Allegri da Correggio (*c*.1489–1534), Italian painter, often credited as the founder of the Lombardian School.

62. *Raphael*: Raphael Sanzio (1483–1520), a highly celebrated Italian painter who is often grouped with the Renaissance figures Michelangelo and Leonardo da Vinci.

63. *And I too am a painter!*: according to a footnote in Thomas Holcroft's English translation of Genlis's *Tales of the Castle* (London: G. Robinson, 1785), Correggio studied a painting by Raphael with great attention and then exclaimed 'Anch' io son pittore' ('I, too, am a Painter'), p. 4, n. 87. The anecdote was repeated widely throughout the 1780s by Martin Sherlock among others. William Hayley refers to it in passing in the Preface to *Triumphs of Temper*, p. vi.

64. *'swift as imagination or the wings of love'*: unknown.

Volume II

1. *'O! sweet to follow nature's powerful voice, / And make the friends of nature friends of choice'*: unknown.

2. *irrevocable chain*: *The Monthly Review* (1787) commented on this phrase thusly: 'What is meant by an 'irrevocable chain', we do not rightly understand. We have heard of *iron chains*, and *golden chains*: we have heard too of *irrevocable decrees*. Should the Lady tell us, that *chain* is used for *decree*, we must observe to her that the *Catachresis* is much too violent, and such as the sober critic can never admit', p. 447.

3. *ensign*: a junior rank of commissioned officer in the navy, a much lower position than Colonel, the rank of Theresa's brother.

4. *'A vermil-tinctur'd lip, / Love-darting eyes, and tresses like the morn'*: from Milton's *Comus* (op. cit.): 'What need a Vermil-tinctur'd Lip for that, / Love-darting Eyes, or Tresses like the Morn?', p. 47.

5. *Handel*: George Frideric Handel (1685–1759), a German-English composer famous for his operas, oratorios, and concerti grossi.

6. *Albert*: the husband of Charlotte, the object of Werther's unrequited love in Goethe's *Werther*.

7. *'Whence is this faintness in my feeble mind? Why has its noble energy decreased?'*: from Canto II of *The Inferno of Dante*, quoted in the notes to the third epistle of Hayley's *Essay on Epic Poetry*: 'And whence this faintness in thy feeble mind? / Why has its noble energy decreas'd', p. 189.

8. *the Circus*: The Circus is a work of Georgian architecture in the city of Bath, begun in 1754 and completed in 1768. The name comes from the Latin 'circus', which means a ring, oval or circle. The most desirable houses were those on the north side, with their sunny south-facing fronts, and were occupied by William Pitt, by then Earl of Chatham and in his second term as Prime Minister, and John, fourth Duke of Bedford. Many occupants were seasonal visitors from London.

9. bound by no vows: i.e. unmarried. We soon learn that the secret admirer is Frank Hyde.

10. *'That heart is ever lightly priz'd ...Who yields her love too soon'*: from Thomas Percy's *The Hermit of Warkworth; a Northumberland Ballad. In three fits of cantos* (London: T. Davies, and S. Leacroft, 1771): 'That heart, she said, is lightly priz'd, / Which is too lightly won; / And long shall rue that easy maid, / Who yields her love too soon', p. 20.

11. *'Whoso sheddeth the blood of man, by man shall his blood be shed'*: 'Whoso sheddeth man's blood, by man shall his blood be shed: for in the image of God made he man' (Genesis 9:6).

12. *'Fancy augments the dangers of the deep, / And expectation loads the wing of time'*: The British Museum has an engraved drawing of two young women sitting together at the edge of a grassy cliff overlooking the sea. Entitled 'Expectation', it has the inscription: 'To bosoms heaving & to Eyes that weep / While lovers linger in a distant clime / Fear multiplies the dangers of the deep / And expectation loads the wing of time'. Designed by Henry William Bunbury and engraved by John Raphael Smith, it was published in London on 1 January 1784. The theme joining this image and *The Victim of Fancy* is the anguish of waiting for loved ones to come home from sea. But broadly speaking the writing is somewhat conventional. A similar phrasing is used in John Hoy junior's 'Delia's Farewel, an elegy', which was collected in his *Poems on Various Subjects* (Edinburgh: Macfarquhar and Elliot, 1781): 'Save where my absent friend, by fancy seen, / Augments the horrors of my tortur'd breast', p. 54. *Elfrida, a dramatic poem* (London: J. and P. Knapton, 1752) by

William Mason has 'With what a leaden and retarding weight, / Does Expectation load the wing of Time?', p. 12.

13. *'the grey dawn and the pleiades'*: from John Milton's *Paradise Lost*: 'the gray / Dawn, and the Pleiades before him danc'd / Shedding sweet influence', book VII, ll. 373–5.

14. *It is now three years only … walls of superstition*: another reference to her incarceration in a nunnery.

15. The Progress of Fashion: *The Progress of Fashion: exhibiting a view of its influence in all the departments of life* (London: J. Sewell, 1786).

16. *to try the bath*: a reference to the notionally recuperative powers of the spa waters at Bath.

17. *'Those snarling and satirical tempers… every cut of whose tongue is like the stab of a poniard, find the unworthy abuse they make of talents, so estimable when rightly applied, goes not unpunished: as they spare none, so none spare them; and, were they at the highest top of exaltation, the lowest mortal upon earth would think he had a right to fall upon them, and to rob them of the good qualities they otherwise have'*: Baltasar Gracián, *The Hero*, translated by 'a gentleman of Oxford' (London: T. Cox, 1726): 'For, not to mention those that squander it away, as Prodigals do their Money, how many do we see that employ it to very vile Purposes; those snarling and satyrical Tempers I mean, every Cut of whose Tongue is like the Stab of a Poinard [*sic*] to the Breast. But the unworthy Abuse they make of this so estimable a Talent, when rightly applied, goes not unpunish'd; as they spare none, so none spare them; insomuch that were they at the highest top of Exaltation, the lowest Mortal upon Earth wou'd think he had a Right to fall upon them, and to rob them even of good Qualities they otherwise have', pp. 27-8. A poniard is a lightweight dagger.

18. *This is the last time that I shall write to you … THERESA MORVEN*: the novel has a "happy ending" here, with Theresa anticipating the arrival of her 'beloved brother'. But the book continues with Ruth's narrative and other interpolations, as the fairytale ending is unravelled.

19. *They travelled by easy stages to Portsmouth*: major port on the south coast, about 80 miles south-east of Bath.

20. *the gallant Ercilla*: Don Alonso de Ercilla (1533–94). See also the third epistle of Hayley's *Essay on Epic Poetry*: 'The brave ERCILLA sounds, with potent breath, / His Epic trumpet in the fields of death', ll. 239–40. According to Hayley's notes in *Essay on Epic Poetry*, Ercilla was 'equally distinguished as a Hero and a Poet', p. 207.

21. *'These, by their efforts in the dread debate … And fixed it on the brow of faint Despair'*: taken from Hayley's extended excerptions from Ercilla in the notes to the third epistle, *Essay on Epic Poetry*: 'He, by his efforts in the dread debate, / Forc'd the determin'd will of adverse Fate, / From shouting Triumph rush'd the palm to tear, / And fix'd it on the brow of faint Despair', p. 224.

22. *meed*: according to the *Oxford English Dictionary*, in early usage it meant something given in return for labour or service; wages, hire; recompense, reward, deserts; a gift. Later usage: a reward or prize given for excellence or achievement; a person's deserved share of praise, honour, and so on.

23. *'From her slack hand the garland she had wreath'd / Down dropt – and all its faded honours shed: / Speechless she stood and pale!'*: an adaptation of lines in Milton's *Paradise Lost*: 'From his slack hand the garland wreath'd for Eve / Down dropt, and all the faded roses shed: / Speechless he stood and pale, till thus at length / First to himself he inward silence broke', book IX, ll. 892–5.

24. *the gallant Curtis*: Admiral Sir Roger Curtis, first baronet (1746-1816), an officer of the British Royal Navy. Curtis served during the American Revolutionary War and the French Revolutionary Wars and was highly praised in the former conflict for his bravery under fire at the Great Siege of Gibraltar. See *The Gallant Captain (now Sir Roger) Curtis, nobly Exerting himself in Saving the lives of the drowning Spaniards, after the Destruction of their Gun Boats, before Gibraltar, on the memorable 13th Sepr 1782*, reproduced in George Frederick Raymond, *A New, Universal and Impartial History of England* (London: 1787?)

25. *'Ye blossoms of nature, ye dews of the morn ... I could die and petition no more'*: this appears to be, as the text implies, an original composition by the author.

26. *'Who was in life but as a dream to me'*: from Camoens's 'Sonnet LXXII', quoted in Hayley's *Essay on Epic Poetry*, pp. 276–7.

27. *'Without or infamy or fame, / Close the blank business of this mortal scene'*: from Canto III of *The Inferno of Dante*, quoted in Hayley's *Essay on Epic Poetry*: 'All who without or infamy or fame, / Clos'd the blank business of their mortal scene!', p. 193.

28. *Michael Bruce*: Michael Bruce (1746–67), a Scottish poet. He was barely twenty-one years old when he died.

29. *'Starting and shiv'ring in the inconstant wind ... And lay me down in peace with them that rest'*: from Michael Bruce's 'Elegy: To Spring', *Poems on Several Occasions* (Edinburgh: J. Robertson, 1770), p. 115.

30. *'The morning will dawn on the night of the grave'*: an allusion, perhaps, to James Beattie's *The Hermit*: 'For morn is approaching, your charms to restore, / Perfumed with fresh fragrance, and glittering with dew / Nor yet for the ravage of winter I mourn; / Kind Nature the embryo blossom will save – / But when shall Spring visit the mouldering urn! / O when shall it dawn on the night of the grave!' This text is taken from *Poems on Several Occasions* (Edinburgh: W. Creech, 1776), p. 83.

31. *'The worm now tastes that rosy mouth... Her snowy bosom loves to lie'*: from the ballad 'Adam and Ellen': 'The worm now tastes that rosy mouth / Where glow'd, short time, the smiles of youth; / And in my heart's dear home / Her snowy bosom loves to lie. / I hear, I hear the welcome cry— / I come, my love, I come'. The lovers have been identified as Adam Fleming and Ellen Irvine and the author as 'E.S.J.', a Scottish poet. This version of the text is taken from the *Scientific Magazine, and Freemasons' Repository* (1797) vol. 1, p. 348.

32. *than breath shut up from a new-folded rose*: from *The Indian Queen: a tragedy. Written by the Honorable Sir Robert Howard, and Mr. Dryden* (London: J. Tonson, 1735): 'A greater Sweetness on these Lips there grows / Than Breath shut out from a new-folded Rose', p. 214. First performed in 1664, the play was expanded with additional music in 1695 by Henry Purcell.

33. *of my lost youth, thou only bride!*: the final stanza of the 'Adam and Ellen' ballad: 'Take, take me to thy lowly side / Of my lost youth thou only bride, / O, me to thy tomb! / I hear, I hear the welcome sound – / Yes, *life can flee at sorrow's wound.* / I come, I come, I come'. This version of the text is taken from *The Scientific Magazine* (op. cit.).

SILENT CORRECTIONS

Volume I

18 sat] set
18 pratler] prattler
24 Embarassed] Embarrassed
24 Mr. Manvill] Mr. Manville
24 staid] stayed
26 trowser-wise] trouser-wise
28 Mr. Manvill] Mr. Manville
28 rout] route
29 forbode] forebode
32 sat] set
35 Dr. C.] Dr. C——
37 stedfastly] steadfastly
38 faultering] faltering
39 intreaties] entreaties
46 incumbered] encumbered

Volume II

66 aukwardly] awkwardly
67 chesnut] chestnut
71 piano forte] pianoforte
72 magination] imagination
79 chilness] chillness
82 the the] the
86 faultering] faltering
90 recal] recall
96 sentimentss] sentiments
99 crouding] crowding
101 faultering] faltering
104 Johanna] Joannah
108 sooth] soothe

For Product Safety Concerns and Information please contact our EU
representative GPSR@taylorandfrancis.com
Taylor & Francis Verlag GmbH, Kaufingerstraße 24, 80331 München, Germany